THIEVING WEASELS

BILLY TAYLOR

DIAL BOOKS

DIAL BOOKS
An imprint of Penguin Random House LLC
375 Hudson Street
New York, NY 10014

Library of Congress Cataloging-in-Publication Data
Names: Taylor, Billy, 1960- author.
Title: Thieving weasels / Billy Taylor.
Description: New York, NY : Dial Books, [2016] | Summary: "Just when Skip O'Rourke thinks he's finally free of his con-artist family, they drag him back to Long Island for one last scam...but nothing about this con is what it seems"—Provided by publisher.
Identifiers: LCCN 2015039465 | ISBN 9780525429241 (hardcover)
Subjects: | CYAC: Swindlers and swindling—Fiction. | Family problem—Fiction. | Identity—Fiction. | Humorous stories. | BISAC: JUVENILE FICTION / Law & Crime. | JUVENILE FICTION / Family / General (see also headings under Social Issues). | JUVENILE FICTION / Humorous Stories.
Classification: LCC PZ7.1.T384 Th 2016 | DDC [Fic]—dc23
LC record available at https://lccn.loc.gov/2015039465

Printed in the United States of America
1 3 5 7 9 10 8 6 4 2

Design by Maya Tatsukawa
Text set in Rotation LT Std

For my parents,
who were nothing like the people in this book

1

I WOULD HAVE KILLED TO GO TO PRINCETON.

Yale, Dartmouth, and Stanford were my top choices, and the universities of Pennsylvania, Michigan, and Texas were my backups. They were all great schools, and I would have been happy to attend any one of them. Or at least I would have until I met Claire. Then the only schools I cared about were Princeton, Princeton, and Princeton, though not necessarily in that order.

Pop Quiz: Did you know F. Scott Fitzgerald went to Princeton? And presidents Woodrow Wilson and Grover Cleveland? Even John F. Kennedy went there, but he couldn't hack it and transferred to some third-rate dump named Harvard. The list of influential Princeton grads is insanely impressive and includes everyone from astronauts and Supreme Court justices to CEOs and Nobel Prize winners. If college was a superhero, Princeton would be Batman. (Sorry, Superman.) If prestige were a sporting event, Princeton would be the Super Bowl. I'm not kidding.

And I'd taken no chances on getting in. I'd read every blog, manual, and how-to guide on the subject, crushed my SATs, and polished my personal essay until it sparkled like a priceless gem. Just as important, I'd made sure my clubs and extracurricular activities were commendable; my sport of choice not-too-obvious or not-too-obscure (lacrosse); and my financial aid form a work of art. In other words, I'd done everything humanly possible to get into Princeton. Then, when there was nothing else left to do, I checked the box for Early Decision, mailed out my application, and waited.

And waited.

A n d . . .

W . . . A . . . I . . . T . . . E . . . D . . .

But here's the thing about applying to a major university. It doesn't matter if you're Prince Albert or Albert Einstein—who once taught at Princeton, by the way—nobody in the admissions office will tell you squat, no matter how much you beg, plead, or threaten. Which in the case of early decision applicants like me, meant one-and-a-half months of pure, undiluted torture. My only solace was that I was not alone. Twenty-one of my classmates at Wheaton Preparatory Academy had applied for early decision to their schools, and for the next six weeks we greeted one another with the same anxious words:

"You hear anything yet?"

The answer was always No, and by Thanksgiving we were twenty-two sleep-deprived zombies. The following week, out of a combination of camaraderie and desperation, we began meeting up in the school mail room to watch—in slow motion and extreme close up—as Mrs. Daulton, Wheaton's million-year-old and molasses-legged mail lady, squinted at each and every piece of mail and slowly, Slowly, SLOWLY, placed it in our slots.

Finally, on December fourteenth, the letters began arriving. There were tears and cheers, hugs and high fives, wishes granted and dreams shattered. But the one thing that didn't arrive was *my* acceptance letter. It was excruciating, and I spent countless hours searching for meaning in my predicament. Was my letter's tardiness a good thing or bad? Did this improve my odds or decimate them? If a Princeton applicant ran into the woods and screamed his head off and nobody heard him, did that make him a complete idiot? I had no idea. All I knew was that by the end of the semester I was the only one left waiting, and I was losing my mind.

"Cam?"

I looked up, and Mrs. Daulton was holding something in her hand. It was white and thin and looked like a letter from a major university. I shot across the room and snatched it from her fingers. The return address read Princeton University, and I swallowed hard.

"Are you going to open it?" she asked.

"I guess I better."

I tore off the side of the envelope, and the first word I saw was "Congratulations."

I was in.

"I knew you could do it," Mrs. Daulton said with a smile.

"Thank you."

I jammed the letter in my backpack and floated out of the mail room on a cloud of victory. All my time, hard work, and anxiety had paid off. Poor, cafeteria-working, trust fund–deprived Cam Smith was going to Princeton, and I didn't even have to kill anyone to do it.

Yet.

2

I COULDN'T WAIT TO CALL CLAIRE AND TELL HER THE NEWS. My shift at the cafeteria had ended early, and when I checked the time on my phone I saw there were five minutes left before her parents were due to pick her up. That was all the time I needed, and I broke into a sprint. Twenty-four hours earlier, I would have crashed into a dozen students wearing Wheaton blazers as I raced across campus, but finals were over, and my classmates were winging their way to Aspen, Taos, and the Caribbean for the holidays. I was spending Christmas in the comfort and splendor of my dorm room, but that hardly mattered because in a few short months I'd be going to Princeton. With Claire.

Or at least I would be if Claire completed her application. She had been putting off writing her personal essay for weeks, and her lack of anxiety about it was giving me anxiety. Not that she had anything to worry about. As a third-generation Princeton legacy with a 3.95 GPA and outstanding SATs, Claire Benson was as close to a slam dunk as there was. Still, legacy or not, all applications had to be postmarked by January first. No exceptions.

I was obsessing over this when I approached the dorms and spotted Claire standing in the parking lot surrounded by suitcases. As a young girl Claire had studied ballet, and with her dancer's poise and brown hair pulled back tight she still resembled the ballerina she'd wanted to be in grade school. God, she was beautiful. And smart. And rich. What she was doing with a scholarship student like me, I had no idea. But I wasn't complaining. Well, except for her not finishing her essay. Otherwise, she was like one of those flawless and dazzling specters you met on the highest level of a video game.

I vaulted over a hedge and was about a hundred yards away from her when the biggest Mercedes I'd ever seen glided into the parking lot, and Ken and Barbie hopped out. Okay, so maybe Claire's parents weren't really named Ken and Barbie, but that's who they looked like—only older and with better skin.

Claire claimed her parents wanted to meet me, but one look at their car, clothes, and diamond-crusted accessories, and I was so intimidated I hid behind an azalea bush. Yes, I know this was 110 percent pathetic, but I'd spent zero time around people like the Bensons, and something told me they would not be impressed by my floppy hair, chipped-tooth smile, and JCPenney attire. Not to mention that at five foot nine, Claire was an inch taller than me—three if she wore heels. Claire swore this wasn't a big deal, but I *knew* it was the first thing people noticed when they saw us together. I kept hoping her parents would dash off for a quick game of tennis and give Claire and me some time alone, but this did not happen. Instead, they loaded up their Mercedes and drove off without so much as a glance in my direction.

Embarrassed at myself and despondent, I climbed out from behind the azalea bush and watched as their taillights grew smaller in the distance. By the time they disappeared, my heart had turned to Jell-O, and there was nothing left to do but trudge back to my room and endure the passing hours until classes resumed in January. I counted every crack in the tiles as I moped down the hallways and every step on the stairs as I climbed to my floor. I was so caught up in my misery I failed to notice that the door to my room was open.

Then I did and froze.

I was certain I had locked it that morning, and there was no reason for someone from Student Services to be inside. But someone *was* inside, and I looked around for a weapon. My only options were a pizza box and an old brass fire extinguisher. Neither would help if the person inside had a gun, and I figured my best bet was the element of surprise. I decided to kick open the door, grab my lacrosse stick, and impale whoever was in there.

It was an excellent plan, and would have worked if my

lacrosse stick had been where I'd left it. Unfortunately, it was not, and before I could think of a Plan B, my legs were knocked out from under me, and I landed on my back with a thud.

"Hello, Skip."

I looked up, and Uncle Wonderful was standing over me with my lacrosse stick in his hands.

"What's this thing?" he asked, pressing the business end of the stick against my throat.

"It's a lacrosse stick," I sputtered.

"What's that? Some fancy new game rich kids play?"

"Lacrosse is actually the oldest team sport played in America. The Plains Indians invented it to prepare for battle."

Uncle Wonderful looked at the stick with newfound respect. "No shit?"

"But enough of a history lesson," I said. "What are you doing here?"

"Taking you home."

I shook my head. "No way. This is my home now."

"Save it. Your mother wants me to bring you back, so I'm bringing you back."

"Why didn't she come herself?" I asked.

"Because she's in Shady Oaks."

"What's that? A retirement home for convicted felons?"

"No, smart guy, it's a mental institution. Your mother tried to kill herself last week."

3

THE FIRST TIME I GOT ARRESTED I WAS FOUR YEARS OLD. Actually, arrested is the wrong word for it. It was more like I was taken into custody. My mother was the one who got arrested, although we both wound up with our pictures in the paper. In the photograph, we're being led out of Macy's in handcuffs and beneath it the caption reads "The Littlest Criminal." Except that was wrong, too. Not the little part, the criminal part. Mom and I were never criminals. Criminals rob banks. Criminals steal cars. Criminals deal drugs. Mom and me? We were weasels. We were thieves. We were slime. And so was everyone else in our family. I'd bet a million dollars there hasn't been one minute in my entire life when at least one of my relatives wasn't collecting welfare under an assumed name. And I'd bet another million there were at least two more cashing disability checks for jobs they never held.

Like I said, we were slime.

The kid in the paper told the police his name was Michael Dillon, but that was an alias. Over the years I've been Bobby, Timmy, Richie, Matthew, Mark, Luke, and John. For a long time I wanted to be called Waldo after the guy in the *Where's Waldo?* books, but my mother said no to that because it would have stood out too much. And in our line of work that's the last thing you want. My real name is Stephen O'Rourke, although I've never seen my birth certificate or any legal proof of my existence. My mother calls me Sonny, and everybody else calls me Skip. The best thing about a nickname is you don't have to change it every time you change your identity, which I've done more times than your average seventeen-year-old has flossed.

Here's how it worked: Mom would lease an apartment under a fake name, pay first and last month's rent, and after that we'd rob the place blind. People were always happy to talk to a jolly fat lady and her cute little boy, and by the end of the first week we'd have learned everything there was to know about everybody who lived there: the hours they worked, when they were gone, and when they were born. After that, it was simply a matter of slipping into their apartments and finding their Social Security numbers. We'd take out credit cards in their names, shopped till we dropped, and sell what was left of their identities for a few hundred dollars. Three months later, and we were on to the next place.

I once asked my mother if she felt guilty for stealing from the people who lived next door.

"Why?" she replied. "It's not like they're family."

Then she'd rip off one of my uncles, and when I asked her about that she'd say, "That's because he's a real A-hole."

I'll say this about my mother: she may have been a cold-hearted thief, but she rarely cursed in my presence.

That said, she did lie about everything. Especially to me, and especially about who my father was. Sometimes he was an Irish tenor. Other times he was a diesel mechanic. Most of the time he was just "some guy." When I asked my Grandpa Patsy about it, he'd just sigh and say, "Talk to your mother. That's her deal, not mine."

So, there you have it. Most kids have a father. I have a deal.

I was seven years old when I started to realize just how messed up my life was. This was a challenging time for Mom and me. My value had always been my size, and as I grew I became a liability. People began to wonder why the kid wandering through the Fragrance Department at Lord & Taylor on a Tuesday afternoon wasn't in school. In other words, they paid *attention* to me—which is something you really don't want when your mother is trying to stuff bottles of Chanel No. 5 in your Buzz Lightyear backpack.

We had two options: I could hang around our apartment all day, or I could go to school. We tried the former, but there are only so many hours a day a seven-year-old boy can watch television, and after I almost burned down the third floor of the Cheshire Arms Apartments, we tried the latter.

The night before my first day of school I was super nervous. With the exception of my cousin, Roy, I had never spent time around kids my own age and didn't know how to act. Was school like jail, where you were supposed to punch out the toughest guy in your cell? Or was it like a convenience store, where you flirted with the lady behind the counter while your mother stole milk and Mylanta? I had no idea.

What surprised me the most about school was how easy it was and how much easier it became. I could barely read when I got there, so they put me in a class with the dumb kids, and let's just say the contrast was more than a little obvious. I had grown up fast-talking sales ladies and policemen while my fellow students could barely wipe their own noses. By the end of the first week I was the star pupil, and by the end of the second I was transferred to a class where, if nothing else, the kids knew which end of a pencil to stick up their noses.

What I liked best about school was the companionship. No one had ever wanted to be my friend before, and overnight a whole new world opened up. I had been living in this alternative universe where playdates, class trips, and just about everything else a seven-year-old boy might enjoy had no value. Sure, my mother stole plenty of nice stuff for me, but even the best toys aren't much fun when you have no one to play with. In school, however, I was just like everyone else, and it was *glorious*.

"Don't get too attached," my mother said when I told

her about my new friends. But I didn't listen and made pals with everyone from the strange kids who smelled like pee all the way up to the principal. I can't tell you how exciting it was to have people I barely knew call me by my name in the halls. Even if it wasn't my real name.

Then the inevitable happened.

"Get your things together," my mother said one Saturday morning.

"Why?" I asked. "I don't have school today."

"We're leaving."

Her words were like a punch in the stomach.

"But I have a test on Monday," I begged. "And Mrs. Fleagler said I could sing the song from *Cats* in music class."

"You can sing in the car. Now grab your stuff and let's go."

That was the day I stopped trusting my mother. After that, I was always careful not to tell her too much about school or my classmates. Is that crazy or what? If I couldn't tell my own mother about my life, then who could I tell?

No one, that's who. And here's the thing about lying: not only is it exhausting to keep a thousand stories and fabrications in your head, it's also incredibly lonely. And I hate being alone. Not to sound overly dramatic, but I left a major chunk of my heart in that elementary school on the day we moved away. I've been trying to get it back ever since.

The only positive thing about my predicament was that I got to keep my textbooks, and by the time my mother got around to enrolling me in a new school I had them memorized. Math, science, and spelling, I knew them backward and forward.

No more classes with dumb kids for me, I told myself. This time it's going to be different.

And for a while it was. I made a point of not telling my mother about school, and on the rare occasions when she did ask, I was careful not to reveal too much. I'm sure my mother knew something was up, but she was a little fuzzy in the head from the grapefruit and tuna fish diet she had started the month before. My mother was always trying some crazy diet, and this one turned her into a complete space cadet. Unfortunately, she zoomed straight back to earth on the night my second grade teacher called.

"What did she want?" I asked when my mother hung up the phone.

"Get packing."

"What?"

"You heard what I said. And if you ever do something like this again, I'll break your arm."

"What did I do?" I asked as tears filled my eyes.

"Your teacher said you were the best student she's ever had and wants to put you in a class for gifted students."

"But that's good, right?"

"No, it's *not* good. Gifted students stand out. People remember them. Use your head, Sonny. Two years from now this lady could see your picture in the paper, and we could all wind up in jail."

"I didn't think about it that way."

"Of course you didn't. That's what school does—it makes you stupid. From now on you get only Cs and Bs, and the only exceptional thing I want to hear about you is that you're exceptionally average."

"Okay."

"Good. Now let's get out of here before the National Honor Society tries throwing a car wash in the living room."

I was thirteen years old when I finally had enough, although it wasn't for the obvious reasons. Yes, I was sick of the lying, and the loneliness, and the constant moving around. Yes, I was sick of my mother, and my family, and the never-ending stream of disgusting apartments. Yes, I was sick of acting stupid, and conning my classmates, and throwing tests. I was sick of it all, but I would have kept on going because it was the only life I knew.

My mother always said ordinary people were stooges—chumps and goody-goodies who slaved away at crummy jobs, had no hope, and owed their souls to the credit card companies. She said we were above all that. We lived where we wanted, did what we wanted, and took what we wanted. We were free.

But were we really free? Between the lies, and scams, and never-ending fear of getting busted we put in as many hours as the next guy, except we had a lot less to show for our effort. Think about it. Here I was thirteen years old, and I'd never played Little League baseball. I'd never joined Boy Scouts. I'd never had a best friend, or slept on the same mattress for more than a couple of months. It was crazy. The only taste of real life I saw was in the empty apartments of the people I robbed. It was pathetic. *I* was pathetic, and I yearned for something better.

The opportunity came, like everything else in my life, through a jimmied window.

One of the most common residents in every apartment complex where Mom and I lived was the newly divorced dad. Growing up, I saw literally hundreds of them shuffling down hallways and carrying bags of Chinese takeout and convenience store beer. They rarely had anything worth stealing—alimony and child support took care of that—but I still enjoyed breaking into their apartments and pouring stale beer down the back of their TV sets. Yes, I knew this was a really mean thing to do, but I couldn't help myself. There was something about these losers that made me so incredibly angry. It must have been because they had everything I wanted out of life—a real house, home-cooked meals, birthdays at Chuck E. Cheese—and threw it all away. It made absolutely no sense to me.

All that changed on the afternoon I slipped into some ex-husband's apartment and came across what can only be described as a *shrine* to Wheaton Preparatory Academy. I'm not exaggerating when I say the entire place was covered, floor to ceiling, with every type of pennant, banner, and poster imaginable, as well as dozens of photos of football, baseball, and lacrosse teams. Creepy doesn't begin to describe it, and right in the middle of this sea of crimson and blue—like it was the single greatest achievement in this poor schnook's life—was his Wheaton diploma. In eight years of breaking into apartments I'd never seen anything like it.

My first impulse was to tear the place to shreds. Just yank every piece of Wheaton memorabilia off the walls and rip it into teeny-tiny pieces. Except I couldn't. It would have been like cutting out the man's heart.

Instead, I slipped out the window (without touching the TV, I might add) and headed straight to the library to find out about this Wheaton place. It was dark outside when I was finished, and my eyes burned from having read so much, but I was sure of two things:

1. I really wanted to go to Wheaton Academy.
2. I'd have to run away from my family to do it.

4

WE WERE THIRTY MILES SOUTH OF ALBANY WHEN THE STATE trooper's lights appeared in the rearview mirror.

"We have a visitor," I said, gripping the steering wheel tighter.

Uncle Wonderful glanced out the back window. "So we have."

"What do you want to do?" I asked.

"What do you mean?"

"What's our play? Is this car stolen?"

"I can't seem to remember."

"Stop messing around," I said. "I'm using my good name here."

Uncle Wonderful yawned. "You're a big boy. You figure it out."

This was why Uncle Wonderful had wanted me to drive,

I realized. It was a test. I eased the car onto the shoulder and held out my hand.

"Okay," I said. "Give me your insurance card and registration, and if you try anything funny I'm telling the trooper you abducted me. I'll say I was getting money from a cash machine, and you put a gun to my head. There are at least ten people at Wheaton who will vouch for me, and two of them are retired judges. Who's going to vouch for you, Uncle Wonderful? Your parole officer?"

The grin dropped from his face, and he handed over the registration and insurance card without a word. The paperwork said the car belonged to a Mr. Phillip Boylan of 421 Leprechaun Lane, Sayville, New York. The print job looked real, but the address was a joke. Leprechaun Lane? Why didn't he just put down Impossible to Believe Lane?

I eyed the sideview mirror as the trooper climbed out of his cruiser. Normal mothers tell their kids they have only one chance to make a first impression; weasel moms tell theirs they only have one chance to size up a mark. The trooper put on his hat, and the first thing that struck me was his air of regimented formality. This said ex-military. More than that, his back was so straight you could have used it to draw a vector in geometry class. This said ex-Marine, and I knew my play. When the trooper got within a few feet of the car, I turned to Uncle Wonderful and yelled, "I don't care what you say! When we get home I'm heading straight to the recruiting office and signing up!"

It took Uncle Wonderful less than a second to catch on. “The hell you are,” he yelled back.

“It’s what Dad would have wanted!”

“But your dad’s not here anymore, is he?”

I waited until the trooper was next to my window and said, “That’s right. He gave his life for this country so bums like you can criticize the people who put their very lives on the line for it.”

“License, registration, and proof of insurance, please,” the trooper growled.

I whipped my head around and shouted, “What?” The trooper’s eyes doubled in size, and before he could say another word I clapped a hand to my forehead. “Oh my God! I’m sorry, Officer. My uncle and I are arguing about me joining the Marines, and I kind of lost my head. Was I speeding or something?”

“License, registration, and proof of insurance, please.”

I handed over the paperwork, and the trooper marched back to his cruiser to run it through the computer. I figured the odds were fifty-fifty I’d be eating dinner in a jail cell.

“Why are you doing this to me?” I asked.

“You broke your mother’s heart. It’s only fair.”

“Fair? And it’s fair that you people won’t leave me alone?”

“You people?” he replied in disgust. “We’re your family, Skip. We’re all you’ve got.”

I thought about Claire and the life I’d created at Wheaton and said, “No, you’re not. You’re not even close.”

I glanced in the rearview mirror and tried to visualize what the trooper had seen when I handed over my license. Did he see the youngest member of a family of thieves, or just some skinny kid with a chipped front tooth and hair in need of a trim? I was hoping for the latter.

"Who's Phillip Boylan?" the trooper asked, returning to the window.

"That would be me," Uncle Wonderful replied.

"Do you know you have a taillight out, Mr. Boylan?"

"I'm sorry, Officer. I lent the car to my nephew here so he could drive girls around at the fancy school he goes to in Schuylerville."

"Wheaton Academy?"

"That's the one."

The trooper looked at my license. "Seventeen years old. That makes you, what? A senior?"

"That's right," I said.

"And you'd rather join the Marines than graduate?"

"Yes, sir."

He looked me up and down and said, "Joining the Corps is no picnic, son. It's a major commitment."

"I know. My father told me all about it."

"Where did he serve?"

"A bunch of places: Haiti, Honduras, Djibouti. But he died in the Korangal Valley."

"Afghanistan?"

I nodded. "Five years ago next month. He was a hero."

"I'm sure he was."

The trooper handed back the paperwork. "Good luck with your decision, but if you want the advice of an old Marine, I'd finish school first. The Corps will still be there in June."

"Yes, sir."

He glanced at Uncle Wonderful. "And you get that taillight fixed."

"You got it, Officer."

The trooper headed back to his cruiser, and Uncle Wonderful laughed. "Djibouti? Where the hell's Djibouti?"

"Africa."

"Never heard of it. How'd you know that guy was a Marine?"

"His posture. Only Marines move like that. And ballet dancers, but he didn't look like a ballerina to me."

Uncle Wonderful nodded. "You always were fast on your feet, Skip."

"So? Did I pass the test?"

"With flying colors."

"Good." I adjusted the rearview mirror and said, "Damn, that trooper's coming back."

Uncle Wonderful turned to look and when he was halfway there I punched him in the jaw.

"Son of a bitch!" he screamed.

"Don't talk that way about my mother," I said. "And the next time you try something when I'm using my good name you'll get a lot worse than that."

• • •

So, what's a good name? A good name is an escape hatch. An emergency exit. A ticket out. In other words, it's the cleanest, safest, most bulletproof fake identity there is. My Grandpa Patsy used to say that if a good name came in a box there'd be a sign on the front reading, "Use only in emergencies." But good names don't come in boxes. In fact, good names don't come anywhere anymore. The computer-controlled, interwoven world we live in has taken care of that, and soon the only name you'll ever have is the name you were born with. Law enforcement types sleep well at night knowing this is the case, but I find it sad and even a little un-American. This country was founded on the possibility of new beginnings, and guys like me have been using good names since the Pilgrims landed on Plymouth Rock.

My good name is Cameron Michael Smith—Cam to my friends. The real Cam Smith was born on April 26, 1995, and died nine months later from a lung infection. That would have been the end of him, but Grandpa Patsy knew a guy in the Schenectady County records office who was in charge of scanning death certificates into their fancy new computer system. For a hundred bucks and a bottle of Bushmills the guy accidentally forgot to scan Cam Smith's death certificate, and it was like the poor kid had never died. After that, we applied for a passport and Social Security card in Cam Smith's name, and just like that I was a whole new person. This was a very popular technique back in the day, and for years our family picnics were filled with dozens of relatives with unscanned birth certificates who were making a nice living cashing checks from every state and federal agency there was. But like I said, computerized record-keeping has put an end to all that.

Good luck and vigilance is the key to every good name. Or, in the case of Mr. and Mrs. Bradley Smith, bad luck and vigilance. Not long after the death of their only son, the Smiths were killed in a car accident. Mrs. Smith was behind the wheel, and the police listed the cause of death as driving while intoxicated. But I think Mrs. Smith died of a broken heart. On nights at Wheaton when I couldn't sleep, I sometimes wondered if the Smiths were looking down on me. If they were, I hoped they were proud because I was taking excellent care of their son's legacy: I had a 3.92 GPA, averaged 1.4 points per game in lacrosse, and wrote smart and funny pieces for the *Weekly Wheatonian*. Plus, I'd just been accepted to Princeton University. I don't mean to brag, but thanks to me Cam Smith had a very bright future ahead of him. Or at least he did until my family came along and messed up his life.

Or should I say, messed up *my* life.

5

"SO, HERE'S THE DEAL," UNCLE WONDERFUL SAID THREE hours later as we drove through the entrance to Shady Oaks Psychiatric Hospital in beautiful Amityville, Long Island. "Your mother's here under the name Sheila O'Rourke, and I'm her brother, Phillip O'Rourke. Her husband's dead, I'm divorced, and we're her only family."

"Why are you using our real names?"

"It's a Medicaid deal. And remember, no matter what happens, don't mess things up. I went through hell getting your mother into this place."

"Who am I supposed to be?" I asked.

"You're her no-good, piece-of-shit son, Skip."

"No, I mean for the story."

"You're her no-good, piece-of-shit son, Skip."

I resisted the urge to punch Uncle Wonderful a second time and gazed out the window. As its name implied, Shady

Oaks really was filled with lots of shady oaks and looked like it had once been part of some grand old estate. If I squinted my eyes and ignored the freaky people wandering around like a pack of drugged-out zombies, it would have been hard to distinguish it from a small upstate college.

I scanned the grounds for my mother, and Uncle Wonderful said, "Don't bother. She's not allowed outside by herself."

"Why?"

"Because she tried to kill herself, and they don't want her trying it again. It kind of screws up their batting average when stuff like that happens."

To be honest, I didn't believe my mother tried to kill herself. I know this is a terrible thing for a son to say, but after a lifetime of cons, scams, and lies, I'd learned to be skeptical of anything my mother said or did. Fool me once, shame on you. Fool me a hundred times, and you're invited to the family reunion. Still, the possibility that my mother needed to be in a mental hospital freaked me out, and on the drive down I was haunted by an image of her strapped to a steel bed and screaming her lungs out. Shady Oaks seemed like a nice place on the outside, but who knew what kind of evil lurked behind its padded walls once the sun went down. I took a deep breath and tried to calm myself.

"Here we are," Uncle Wonderful said, easing into a parking space. He reached under his seat and pulled out a carton of Camel Lights. "These are for your mother."

"Aren't you coming in with me?"

"No, I gotta go see a guy about something."

"You coming back?"

"In an hour. After that, I'll take you to the house."

"What house?"

"Everything in due time, young Skipper. Now go see your mother. She's waiting for you."

I climbed out of the car, and it felt like the weight of the world had descended upon my shoulders on the drive down. Maybe I was only fooling myself, but I really did believe I had escaped from my family. No more lies, no more moving around, no more checking the rearview mirror every thirty seconds. I was just plain old Cam Smith, and for the first time in my life I felt like a normal human being. Then, bam, Uncle Wonderful shows up, and I'm Skip O'Rourke, the no-good, piece-of-shit son of Sheila O'Rourke. God, I hated my family.

I walked into the O'Neil Pavilion and gave my name to the woman at the desk. She made a call and said it would take a few minutes for someone to "fetch" my mother. I tried not to think about where she was being fetched from and leaned against the wall to inspect my mother's new home.

The most surprising thing about the common area at the O'Neil Pavilion was how much it resembled a student lounge at Wheaton. All you needed was a couple of bowls of microwave popcorn and a few million dollars in trust funds, and you wouldn't have been able to tell the two apart.

A skinny patient with bad posture and a scraggly beard looked up from the game show he was watching and stared in my direction. I turned away, but it was too late. He stood up and walked toward me with that slow, zombie-like gait I had seen on all the patients there. Normally, guys like him weren't a problem for me, but getting kidnapped by Uncle Wonderful had thrown me off my game. I pretended to be engrossed in a brochure celebrating the benefits of hand washing, and a moment later he was standing beside me. His eyes were glazed over and bloodshot, and I half-expected him to grab my arm and take a bite out of it. I smiled, and he smiled back, revealing a mouth filled with the most disgusting yellow teeth I had ever seen.

"Hi, cuz," he said in a slow Southern drawl.

"Uh, hi," I said, trying not to stare at his teeth.

"Gotta smoke?"

"Sorry, I don't smoke."

"Then what are those for?" He pointed toward my waist.

I looked down and saw the carton of Camel Lights in my hands.

"Oh yeah, I forgot."

I tried to open the carton, but my fingers were suddenly slippery. I glanced up and Yellow Teeth was staring at me like I was a moron. Out of frustration, I tore the carton in half and a couple of packs fell to the floor. I picked them up and tried to open one, but I couldn't do that either.

"Just one?" Yellow Teeth asked. There were streaks of brown mixed with the yellow, and I could feel my forehead blossoming sweat. "Gotta whole carton there, cuz. One pack won't make a diff."

At this point, I would have handed over a kidney to make him go away. I held out a pack, and he grabbed it out of my hands in a flash. He opened the wrapper with a diamond cutter's precision and pulled out a cigarette.

"Light?"

"Uh . . . no."

Yellow Teeth shuffled over to the desk, and without lifting her eyes from the paperback in her hands, the nurse raised a disposable lighter on a chain and lit his cigarette. He took a long drag, blew the smoke at a No Smoking Past This Point sign, and sauntered back to his game show like I no longer existed.

Anger shot up my spine, and I glared at the nurse with such intense hatred I thought I might burst into flames. Didn't she see that a dangerous psychopath had just forced me to hand over an entire pack of my mother's cigarettes? Why hadn't she tried to stop him? I turned back toward the lounge and was surprised to see that Yellow Teeth was at least two inches shorter than me. It didn't make sense. Seconds earlier, he had seemed like an evil giant. I felt lame and embarrassed and in no condition to see the woman I'd run away from almost four years earlier. Needless to say, this was the precise moment an orderly brought my mother through the door.

The first thing I noticed was how much weight she had lost. Fifty pounds at least. It looked like she'd been hit by a bus. Grooming and fashion were never my mother's top priorities, but she looked worse than I thought possible. Her hair was gray and slumped to one side, her fingernails were bitten to nothing, and her eyes were glazed over and red. But what really freaked me out was the way she moved. For as long as I could remember my mother bounded into every room with complete confidence, but now, as she shuffled toward me, it was like she was afraid the floor was going to collapse beneath her feet. What had happened to her?

"Sonny," she slurred. "C'meeeere and give your mother a hug."

I did as I was told, and it was like hugging an ashtray. Then she tickled my ear like she did when I was a little boy, and my defenses broke down and I felt terrible in a hundred different ways, but mostly because I had doubted she was ill. From the moment Uncle Wonderful appeared in my room, I'd been waiting for the scam to present itself. Except this was no scam. It was my mother, and she was sick.

She broke our hug and stepped back to take a look at me.

"Goodness, Sonny, you're all grown up. And look at that hair."

I ran a hand through my sloppy locks. "You like it?" I asked.

"I like everything about you. Want to go outside?"

"Sure."

"Okay, but you have to sign me out first."

We went to the desk, and my mother introduced me to Valerie, the evil nurse who'd allowed Yellow Teeth to steal my cigarettes. It turned out Valerie was actually quite nice and seemed to care for my mother a lot. So much for first impressions. She asked if I had any matches, and when I said that I didn't, she offered me a book if I promised not to let my mother keep them when I left.

"It's not like I don't trust her," she assured me. "But it's a rule, and I don't want anyone getting in trouble."

"I understand."

As we walked toward the exit my mother whispered, "Valerie's in the middle of a nasty divorce, and her soon-to-be-ex-husband is a total piece of dog doo. He's got this hotsy-totsy girlfriend and is always late with her child support payments. I told her to get a post office box and have all his mail delivered there. She's already taken out two lines of credit and applied for three credit cards in his name. Just watch, we'll have that SOB bankrupt in no time."

"That's really kind of you, Ma, helping out a poor divorcee like that."

"We girls have to stick together."

I reached for the door, and the automatic lock buzzed before my hand even touched the handle. I nodded thanks to Valerie, and out of the corner of my eye spotted Yellow Teeth clutching his pilfered pack of Camel Lights.

"Just a second," I said, and strolled back to the lounge. I held up a half carton of cigarettes and said, "Hey, buddy, you want these?"

Yellow Teeth's eyes grew wide and he stood up. "Sure thing, cuz."

I held out the carton with one hand, and when he reached for it I grabbed the pack of cigarettes from his fingers with the other.

"Hey," he shouted. "Those were mine!"

"No, they weren't," I said with a smile. "You only borrowed them."

6

UNCLE WONDERFUL PICKED ME UP AN HOUR LATER. I DIDN'T bother asking where he'd been because he would have lied about it.

"She looked good," I said as we drove down a suburban street.

"She looks like crap."

"I mean, yeah, but still . . ."

"But still what?"

"I don't know. I'm still trying to process it all."

"What's to process? You broke her heart, and she tried to kill herself. End of story."

"You can't blame that on me," I said. "It's been almost four years since I left. There's no way it's my fault."

"You think so, huh? Well, think again."

We pulled up to a small gray house with a dried-up

hydrangea bush in the front yard, and Uncle Wonderful turned off the engine.

"Where are we?" I asked.

"Go inside and see for yourself. The key's under the mat."

"No way," I said. "I'm not breaking into somebody's house for you. I'm through with all that."

"It's not somebody's house. It's *your* house."

"What are you talking about?" I asked. "I don't own a house."

"Technically it belongs to your mother, but she bought it for you."

I turned to take a closer look. The house had brown shutters, white window shades, and a green mailbox with the name O'Rourke spelled out in gold press-on letters. It looked real. It looked like a home.

"I don't believe you," I said. "My mother's never owned a house in her life."

"You've been away for a long time, Skip."

Uncle Wonderful was right about that, and now things were happening way too fast. One second I was at Wheaton watching Claire drive into the sunset, and the next I was back on Long Island staring at a house with my name on the mailbox. I needed time to catch my breath.

"The code for the alarm is nine-eight-eight-nine," he said. "And there's a car in the garage with the keys in the ignition. It's all legit. Or at least legit enough to pass inspection. You know how to get back to Shady Oaks from here, right?"

"Sure," I replied, unable to take my eyes off the house.

"Visiting hours are nine to eleven in the morning and five to nine at night. I've got things to do tomorrow morning, but I'll drop by around six and I expect to see you there."

I climbed out of the car and walked toward the house. *My* house.

"Oh, and Skipper."

"Yeah?"

"Welcome home."

The key was under the mat just like he said it would be, and the code for the alarm really was 9889. If it wasn't my house, at least Uncle Wonderful's information was accurate. Then I turned on the lights and couldn't believe what I saw. The room was like a mash up of every apartment where my mother and I had lived. On the right was the couch from the Dover Hills apartments where I used to watch *SpongeBob SquarePants*, and next to that was the end table from the Carlton Arms where I used to do my math homework. It didn't seem possible, so I got down on my hands and knees and inspected the underside of the table. Sure enough, there was the picture of a mad scientist I'd drawn with a purple crayon back when I was eight years old.

"Where did all this stuff come from?" I asked aloud as I climbed back to my feet. With the exception of a nineteen-inch SONY Trinitron we stole from a Circuit City in Patchogue (watch the loading dock long enough and someone's bound to get sloppy) my mother and I never took anything substantial with us when we moved. Some clothes, my books, and the Trinitron, and that was pretty much it. Yet, here was all this stuff I knew like the back of my hand. It felt like some crazy dream.

Except it wasn't a dream. It was my life.

I was thirsty and more than a little freaked out, so I went into the kitchen for something to drink. I was about to open the refrigerator when my arm froze. The entire appliance was covered, top to bottom, with artwork from my childhood. Finger paintings, connect the dots, silhouettes—it was all there. Even the little sculpture I'd made from seashells and rocks in Miss Shanley's third grade art class. My throat felt funny, and I didn't know whether to laugh, cry, or run.

I left the kitchen and walked to the bedroom where it got even worse. Every badge, ribbon, and award I'd ever won was hanging on the wall. They were all for second and third place because I didn't want to stand out, but they were all mine. As was the shelf of textbooks I'd stolen from the dozens of schools I'd attended. The rest of my stuff was there, too—Game Boys, LEGOs, Transformers, even my Tony Hawk skateboard with the personally autographed deck. Out of curiosity, I pulled back the bedspread and, sure enough, my *Star Wars* sheets were on the bed. It made no sense.

And yet it made perfect sense. Uncle Wonderful had obviously gone back to the apartments where my mother and

I had lived and cleaned them out after we had left. My family had a vast collection of storage lockers all over Long Island filled with things they had stolen, and the stuff that I was now looking at—the memories, relics, and achievements of my childhood—was simply garbage they couldn't sell.

I wandered back into the living room and noticed a bag from the Gap on a chair. I yanked it open and saw it was filled with shirts, jeans, and socks. This must have been Uncle Wonderful's contribution to my homecoming. The "guy" he went to see while I was at Shady Oaks was the Gap. I couldn't figure out how he knew my sizes until I remembered he'd been in my dorm room back at school. Luckily, the only stuff I cared about were the pictures of Claire on my laptop and my favorites were backed up on the school's server. I had a momentary flash of panic when I thought of Uncle Wonderful getting on to my computer, but then I remembered he was so technically inept he needed a forty-page instruction manual just to change a lightbulb.

Thinking of my dorm room made me think of Claire. So much had happened since I'd last seen her, and I wanted to tell her everything. Except I couldn't. Cam Smith—the boy she knew, loved, and occasionally threw snowballs at—was still at Wheaton. Or at least I *hoped* he was still at Wheaton. I'd been gone only a few hours, but I could already feel my family's icy fingers slipping into my brain as they tried to drag me back into their world.

I pulled out my phone to call Claire, but when I went to dial there was a No Service icon flashing. Weird. I looked around for a landline, but there wasn't one, and I walked outside to get better cell service.

Still nothing.

It was too late to visit a Verizon store, so I went back in the house and pretended not to be too freaked out by the surroundings. There was some bologna and Sunny D in the fridge, and I was about to make myself a sandwich when someone pounded on the front door.

"Open up!" they shouted. "It's the police!"

My weasel muscle memory clicked into high gear, and I looked around for an escape route. My first thought was to race out the back door and not stop running until I reached Wheaton. It was only a few hundred miles away, and if I took breaks for just food and water I could make it by the end of vacation. I dove on the floor and crawled across the living room rug. The police usually posted an officer at the back door during a raid, but maybe I'd get lucky.

I didn't see anyone outside and was about to make a run for it when the person at the front door shouted, "C'mon, Skip, we know you're in there. Stop screwing around and open up."

"Oh, for crying out loud," I said, climbing to my feet. I went to the front door and opened it to reveal my cousin, Roy, and his sidekick, Vinny.

"Busted!" Roy said, barging into the house. "I knew you were in here playing Hungry Hungry Hippos."

"I would have been, but I was too busy trying to escape from the police."

"I can't believe you fell for that," Roy said. "What are you? Six years old?"

"I'm just out of practice."

"That's right. Dad said he found you living the good life in some fancy school upstate. I hear rich girls are crazy wild."

"I wouldn't know."

Roy punched my arm and even though he had the physique of a stalk of celery it still hurt like hell. "That's right," he said. "You always were an altar boy. Yo, Vinny, remember the time Saint Skip over here found that twenty-dollar bill outside Hero Palace and gave it to the guy behind the counter in case somebody came back looking for it?"

"Like it was yesterday, bro."

"So, what are you ladies up to?" I asked.

"We're celebrating," Roy replied.

"Celebrating what?"

"My disability came through," Vinny said with a grin.

"You don't look disabled," I said.

Vinny put a finger to his lips and smiled. "Ssh, don't tell anyone."

7

A FEW MINUTES LATER I WAS SLUMPED IN THE BACK OF Vinny's Hummer H2 as Roy cranked up some hip-hop, and Vinny pretended to be a tank commander. The music obliterated all possibility of conversation, which was fine by me considering how awkward it felt hanging out with my cousin again. Roy was only a few years older than me, but he was like a brother and father all rolled up in one larcenous package. It was Roy who had taught me how to fight, how to drive, and how to throw a football. We hung out together at family functions and broke into houses together as kids. We were thick as thieves because that's exactly what we were. And then we weren't, but Roy didn't seem to notice. He was as loyal as a puppy, and when I ran away I probably broke his heart as much as my mother's.

"This thing drives like a truck," Roy shouted.

"That's because it's a freaking military assault vehicle,"

Vinny said, lowering the music. "All you need is a little body armor and an AK-47 and you could drive this bad boy straight through Baghdad."

Roy laughed and ran a hand through his thick black hair. "And that really means something coming from a guy who's never left the tristate area."

"Eat me. Just because you snuck into Canada once for an Oilers game doesn't make you an international man of mystery."

"I'm the most mysterious person in this vehicle, that's for damn sure."

"Oh yeah? What about our friend in the backseat?" Vinny turned to face me. "So, Skip, why'd you take off? Your boys back on the South Shore not good enough for you?"

"No," I said. "That wasn't it."

"Then what was it?" Roy asked. "What was so important that you had to dump your friends and family like a bucket of dead fish?"

I didn't know what to say. Of all the people in the world Roy should have known the answer to that question. Except he didn't. Because unlike me, Roy had never grown a conscience. From the moment he was born, my cousin was happy to steal anything and everything he could carry. He was the son my mother never had.

"It's complicated," I said, trying to explain it in a way Roy would understand. "I guess I wanted to feel like a regular person for a while."

"And how did that work out for you?"

"Okay, I guess."

"Good, because it's time to stop screwing around and get back to work."

His words sounded more like a threat than a suggestion, and I tried to estimate the seriousness of my predicament. My family knew where I lived, what I looked like, and the intimate details of my good name. But what they didn't know—although they thought they did—was *me*. They assumed that since I'd stopped scamming and stealing that I was weak, but it was exactly the opposite. In the years I'd been away I'd learned that honesty, perseverance, and all the rest of that Campfire Girl stuff they looked down upon was real.

It also didn't hurt that I had Claire waiting for me. But how supportive would she be if Roy or Uncle Wonderful told her who I really was? The answer to that question was too painful to think about, which meant I had just two weeks to extract myself from my family's loving embrace before classes resumed in January. I had my work cut out for me.

"Here we are," Roy said.

I looked up from my brooding and glanced out the window. "Where's here?" I asked.

"Shooters," Vinny announced, like we'd just landed in Oz.

"You mean that bar where you guys used to hang out like a million years ago?"

"You mean the bar where we still hang out," Vinny said with a grin. "C'mon, let's go get trashed."

"I can't go in there," I said. "My ID says I'm seventeen."

"Not this one," Roy said, pulling out a New York State driver's license. "Welcome home, my brother."

I took the license and was surprised to see that the picture on it looked just like me. Or at least it did if the person checking IDs was drunk, high, or legally blind.

"There's no way this will pass inspection," I said.

"No worries," Vinny said. "The guy who manages this place is a friend of mine."

We climbed out of the Hummer, and a Taylor Swift song wafted out of the front door of the bar like a bad smell. I followed Roy and Vinny inside, and as my eyes adjusted to the light I was surprised to see that the place looked like a cross between a Hooters and the Country Bear Jamboree. The waitresses all dressed like cowgirls and wore these ridiculous gun belts stocked with liquor bottles instead of bullets. And if that wasn't corny enough, they also carried giant squirt guns that they used to shoot cocktails into their customer's mouths. Hence the name Shooters.

This was my first time inside a real bar, which was kind of ironic considering what an expert I was on fake IDs, but alcohol was strictly forbidden at Wheaton, and as a scholarship student, getting caught with so much as a beer would have gotten me expelled. Not that this was such an Earth-shattering sacrifice on my part. Unlike the majority of my classmates—most of whom had secret stashes of booze in their rooms—I'd never developed a taste for the stuff.

I hung back while Roy ordered beers and was surprised when the bartender didn't ask to see my ID. I guess Vinny really did know the manager.

"Check it out," Roy said, pointing toward a small stage where a blond waitress with a pink cowgirl hat was running a customer's tie around her neck like a boa constrictor.

"How does that feel?" Roy shouted across the bar.

"For twenty bucks an hour plus tips it feels fantastic!" she yelled back.

"Wow," Roy said in awe. "She's good."

Vinny handed out Heinekens, and we took seats near the stage. The waitress had finished messing with the customer's tie and was now engaged in the more serious business of selling a drink called Santa's South Shore Iced Tea. It may have looked like regular iced tea, she told us, but it was jam-packed with gin, vodka, rum, and tequila and was guaranteed to blow the back of our heads clean off. Her pitch worked like magic, and soon every guy in the place was lined up with his mouth hanging open to get booze shot down his throat.

The waitress was getting closer, and as ridiculous as it was to get shot in the mouth with Santa's South Shore Iced Tea, I didn't want to look like a total lightweight in front of my cousin. Unfortunately, all I had was two tens and three singles in my wallet, and I wondered if it was okay to ask her to make change. I'd blown all the money I'd made that fall on Claire's Christmas present and had only fifty dollars left on my debit card until I returned to my job at the cafeteria. Seventy-three bucks. That would have lasted a month at school, but here in the land of twelve-dollar iced teas it was nothing. Note to self: next time you plan on getting kidnapped remember to have more money in the bank.

"Yo, Skip," Vinny shouted. "Check out Mr. Big Spender."

I turned and saw Roy holding out a fifty-dollar bill.

"Are you out of your mind?" I asked.

"I have to get her attention somehow," he replied.

The waitress spotted the money and her face erupted in a huge smile.

"Is that all for me?" she asked.

"You bet it is," Roy replied. "But you have to share the drink with me." He opened wide and when his mouth was so full of iced tea that it poured down his T-shirt, he stood up and kissed the waitress on the mouth. The crowd cheered, and by the time Roy sat down every guy in the bar was holding out some major currency.

"I think you started something," I shouted at Roy.

"I always was a trendsetter."

The waitress cleared at least two hundred dollars by the time she ran out of iced tea, and as she walked off to count her money, Roy stood up and said, "I'm gonna go talk to her. Yo, Vin, if I'm not back in twenty minutes, leave without me."

"You got it."

Roy gave Vinny a high five then leaned over and whispered in my ear, "Swing by my apartment tomorrow afternoon. There's something we need to talk about, and I don't want Vinny to find out about it. Okay?"

I swallowed hard. "Sure."

"Great!" He slapped me on the back and said, "It's good to have you home."

Roy disappeared, and I took a long pull from my Heineken. It tasted gross, but it was cheaper than Santa's South Shore Iced Tea, so I took another sip and pondered Roy's words. The "something" he mentioned was probably a job that he wanted me to be part of. Damn my family. I'd been home less than five hours, and already they wanted me to put on my weasel costume.

"If you don't mind me saying so," Vinny said, pointing toward the stage where a new waitress had begun dancing, "that girl's got way too much junk in the trunk to be shaking her tail feathers for a living."

"That's classy, Vin," I replied. "Real classy."

"You know me. I'm all about the class."

The new waitress was earning just a fraction of what the first waitress had made. The last thing I wanted was a shot of Marci's Magic Margarita, but I felt sorry for her and pulled out a ten and three singles.

"Thanks," she said as she took my money. "What's your name?"

"Thomas Jefferson. What's yours?"

"Desirée."

"That's a nice name, Desirée. What do you do when you're not shooting people in the face with overpriced cocktails?"

"Change diapers," she said, and danced away.

"Hey," I called after her.

Desirée turned around, and I held out the last of my cash.

"Here," I said. "Buy your kid something nice for Christmas."

8

THERE ARE MANY THINGS TO LOOK FORWARD TO IN LIFE. Your first bike, your first kiss, your first Yankees' game . . .

Your first hangover is not one of them.

I drank half as much as Vinny, but that was more than enough to transform my bed into a Tilt-A-Whirl, and my head into a pulsating pain machine. No matter which way I turned, I felt like I was going to vomit, and when I switched off the lights it only got worse. Finally, out of desperation, I untangled myself from the sheets and crawled to the bathroom.

"This suuuuuucks," I moaned as an entire night's worth of beer and tequila came gurgling up along with the Double Baconator I'd inhaled at Wendy's on the way home. Even worse, I'd put the food on my debit card, and now had less than forty dollars to my name. At least I told them to hold the onions on the Baconator.

When there was nothing left to puke up, I slid down to the floor. The bathroom tile felt cool against my cheek, but my head still felt like the inside of a bouncy castle. *Why do people drink if they end up feeling like this?* I wondered as I curled up with the blue shag pee-pee-protector in front of the toilet. I closed my eyes and passed out swearing I'd never have another drink for as long as I lived.

The next thing I knew it was morning and sunlight was blasting through the windows. The throbbing in my head was still there, and I struggled to my feet to take a look at myself in the mirror. It was a toss-up which was worse: my hair, my eyes, or the imprint of the pee-pee-protector on my cheek. I threw some water on my face and looked around for some aspirin. There was nothing in the Skip O'Rourke Memorial bathroom, so I went into my mother's room to see if I could find some. Her nightstand was empty, and when I opened her medicine cabinet I stepped back in horror. Every inch of it was jammed with prescription medication. And I mean *every* inch. I didn't recognize the names on the bottles, but they all had pictures of drowsy men printed on them along with warnings not to drive or operate heavy machinery after ingesting.

I sat on the edge of the bathtub and tried to remember if my mother had always been a drug addict. I recalled plenty of trips to drugstores, but those were mostly for Whitman Samplers or the Jean Naté cologne she splashed on herself when she didn't feel like taking a bath.

No, the drugs were a recent development. And even though I didn't buy Uncle Wonderful's story that this was ALL MY FAULT, if I had been home I might have been able to stop it.

"I'm sorry, Mom," I said to the shelves full of pills. "I didn't mean for things to turn out this way. I swear I didn't."

The pills didn't reply, and I spent the next few minutes searching for aspirin, Advil, or rat poison. When I couldn't find any of those, I grabbed the least lethal-looking pill in my mother's arsenal and washed it down with tap water. It kicked in while I was in the shower, and I felt so much better I was tempted to take another. But I decided against it. The last thing I needed was to get hooked on pain pills. Not to mention that the gentle throbbing at the base of my skull would be a potent reminder to never drink again. Ever.

Roy and Vinny had abducted me before I'd had a chance to check out the car in the garage, and now I was curious. My mother had zero interest in automobiles, and I expected to find some old beater like the rusted-out Monte Carlo or puke-green Buick she drove when I was a kid. You can imagine my surprise when I walked into the garage and found a brand-new Mustang GT sitting there. And by new I mean there were less than fifty miles on it.

I climbed into the car and took a deep breath. The smell of Armor All and leather tickled my nostrils, and I could picture myself tearing up the roads behind Wheaton. Underclassmen weren't allowed to have cars, but seniors were, and most of my classmates had returned that fall with major motor vehicles. Along with my scholarship and job in the cafeteria, my lack of a car was another brick in the status wall separating me from the other students. My biggest fear was that Claire would dump me for some jerk with a Porsche. A Mustang GT, however, was a perfectly acceptable Wheaton mobile—especially a black one with a retractable moon roof and custom detailing.

The clock on the dash read seven forty-five, which gave me a little more than an hour to take my new ride for a spin before visiting hours at Shady Oaks. I pushed the garage door opener and turned the key in the ignition. The engine roared to life, and I could almost hear a couple of real mustangs frolicking around under the hood. I put the car in gear and began backing out.

I was halfway down the driveway when I spied *O'Rourke* on the mailbox and hit the brakes.

"What are you doing?" I asked out loud. "This car isn't for school. This car is to keep you here. Just like this house and—"

Just like my mother trying to kill herself.

My chest pinched tight, and if I had any brains I would have started running at that very moment. Yes, I would have had to kiss Claire, Wheaton, and Princeton good-bye—not to mention my good name—but I was only seventeen years old and had plenty of time to come up with a new identity. My mistake had been to stay close to home. I should have left New York State entirely and relocated to a place where my family had no connections. Utah, Canada, Europe—the world was full of cities where I could have disappeared forever.

Why didn't I run away? It wasn't the Mustang, and it wasn't the house. It wasn't even my mother trying to kill herself. It was more like all that stuff mashed together. That, plus a false sense of confidence. Deep down, I totally believed I could beat my family at their own game. So I fired up the Mustang and spent the next hour tooling around the Long Island Expressway and pretending to be free of them all.

"Where the hell have you been?" Uncle Wonderful hissed when I pulled into the Shady Oaks parking lot. He was standing there waiting for me.

"Driving around," I said. "Why?"

"Because you were supposed to be here two hours ago. Your mother is waiting for you."

"But visiting hours don't start for another three minutes."

"Wrong, smart guy. Visiting hours *end* in three minutes."

"But the clock on the dashboard says 8:57."

"I don't care what the clock in your car says. Don't you own a watch?"

"I use the clock on my cell phone, but it's messed up right now so I didn't think to look at it."

"Then un-mess it. Your mother needs you."

"I'm sorry."

“Save it,” he said, and opened the door to his car.

“Wait a minute,” I said, getting in his face. “I didn’t ask for this. You were the one who showed up in my dorm room yesterday.”

Uncle Wonderful grabbed a fistful of my hair and smashed my head against the doorjamb. “Listen up, you little turd. Your mother’s in this place because of you, so don’t go telling me that you didn’t ask for it. You want to go back to that rich kid’s playground upstate? Then you give your mother a reason to go on living. Otherwise, I’ll screw up your deal faster than you can say Jack Robinson, and your good name will be so dirty you wouldn’t want to wipe your ass with it. You hear me?”

“Yeah.”

Then he squeezed my mouth open and jammed a cotton swab down my throat. I gagged and pulled away.

“What was that all about?” I coughed.

“DNA,” he said, jamming the swab in a test tube. “It’s better than fingerprints and totally admissible in court. You cross me again, and who knows where this stuff might turn up?”

“Give me a break,” I said.

“I just did. And from now on you show up when you’re supposed to, you leave when you’re supposed to, and you do whatever it takes to make your mother happy. Got it?”

“Happy, huh? Is that why you fed her all those pills, Uncle Wonderful? To keep her happy?”

“I have no idea what you’re talking about,” he said.

"Don't lie to me! I saw your name on some of those prescription bottles."

"Your mother was in pain."

"Then give her an aspirin, not a truckload of pharmaceuticals."

"You weren't here."

"Well, I'm here now and I'm emptying that medicine cabinet as soon as I get home. And if you feed her so much as a Benadryl—DNA or no DNA—I swear to God I'll tear your throat out. Got it?"

He glared at me.

"Good," I said, climbing into the Mustang. "Now, if you'll excuse me, I gotta go see a guy about getting my phone fixed."

9

UNCLE WONDERFUL'S THREAT BURNED IN MY BRAIN AS I marched into the Verizon store. I figured the chances of him doing something funny with my DNA were somewhere between eighty and a million percent, and I weighed the options of going after him before he went after me. A preemptive strike wasn't my style, but what other choice did I have? It wasn't like my family had an appeals committee, and now that Grandpa Patsy was dead, Uncle Wonderful was our de facto leader. He wasn't the oldest, brightest, or best thief in our little clan, but nobody else wanted the job, and that left him in charge. He'd always been a jerk, and nobody loved him the way they loved Grandpa Patsy, but nobody wanted to see him go to prison either. I guess the big question was what would Roy or my mother do to me if I sent him there?

"Can I help you, sir?"

I stepped up to the counter and handed the Verizon rep my phone. "This thing worked fine yesterday when I was upstate, but as soon as I got down here it totally died."

"I'm sorry to hear that, sir. Let's see if we can figure out what the problem is."

I gave him my phone number, and as he looked up my account I said, "It's been a while since I reviewed my plan, but I'm pretty sure I have the one where you can call from anywhere in the United States."

"Your plan isn't the problem, sir. The problem is you owe over eighteen hundred dollars on your account. It's been suspended for lack of payment."

"Eighteen hundred dollars?" I said. "That's impossible."

"I'm afraid not." He spun his terminal around for me to see. "You owe six hundred and fifty-seven dollars for October, five thirty-eight for November, and your December bill is already over seven hundred dollars."

"That's ridiculous. My bill is never more than forty bucks, and I always pay it on time using the kiosk at the Verizon store in Saratoga Springs."

"Did you save your receipts?"

"Of course."

"Good, then let me see those, and maybe we can get to the bottom of this."

"I mean, I don't actually have them here with me. They're in my dorm room upstate."

"I'm sorry, sir. Then, there's nothing I can do about it."

Anger flared inside me. "Listen," I hissed. "I pay my bills, okay?"

"Please lower your voice, sir."

"Why? Will that help you solve my problem?"

"No, but if you don't, I'll have to call the police."

The P word calmed me down right away. "Look," I said in a somewhat less threatening voice, "I'm sorry I shouted at you, but I need that phone. My mother's in a mental institution, and I have to be accessible."

The sales rep leaned in. "Why don't you just buy a Pay as You Go phone. That way you'll at least have a working number until your bill gets straightened out."

I pulled out my debit card. "Fine, give me one of those."

"I'm sorry, but I can't sell you anything until your account is paid in full. I probably shouldn't tell you this, but they carry them at lots of other stores around town."

"Okay, thanks."

After a childhood of crime, few things gave me greater pleasure than paying my bills on time. Verizon had messed up big time, and as soon as I got my hands on those receipts I planned on jamming them down the nearest sales rep's throat. Walgreens carried a disposable phone for seventeen bucks, and that plus fifteen dollars for extra minutes turned my debit card into a pumpkin. I walked outside and dialed Claire before I even got to my car.

"Hey," I said when she answered. "It's me."

"Cam! Are you okay? I've been calling you nonstop since we pulled out of the parking lot yesterday."

"Verizon screwed up my account, and I had to get a temporary phone until they fix my old one."

"Thank God it's just that. I was beginning to think you were abducted by aliens."

"Nope. Just a little institute of higher learning named Princeton University."

"You got in!" Claire shrieked so loud I thought she was going to blow out the earpiece of my new phone. "That's so freaking fantastic! When did you find out?"

"Right after you left."

"Oh man! I'm sorry I wasn't there to celebrate with you."

"Me too. This place is like a prison without you. Can you believe it's only been twenty-four hours since you left? It feels like a week."

"More like a month. My mother's driving me bananas and keeps bugging me to clean my room so she can donate all my stuff to the Junior League rummage sale."

"Isn't your mother a little old to be in the Junior League?"

"Only by a couple of decades. And you won't believe how competitive she is about it. Last year she even bought a ton of stuff on eBay so she'd have the best items to donate."

"That's nuts! And speaking of things that are nuts, why the hell haven't you written your Princeton essay yet?"

"I'm practically finished. Do you want to read it?" she asked.

"Of course I do."

"Great. I'll e-mail it to you right now."

I glanced around the Walgreens parking lot, but didn't see a place to check my e-mail. "Actually," I said, "I was just about to take the bus to Saratoga Springs and deal with Verizon. Can I do it later?"

"Oh. Okay, sure. I just thought you might want to check your e-mail *now*." Then after a dramatic pause added, "But maybe you're not that interested in the Possibility of Expulsion."

"The Possibility of Expulsion?" I said, unlocking my Mustang. "Give me ten minutes."

"Great! And don't worry about your phone."

"Why?"

"You'll see," she said, and hung up.

The Possibility of Expulsion was our secret code for the next stage of our relationship. According to the Wheaton handbook, students caught having sex were subject to all sorts of disciplinary measures, including "the Possibility of Expulsion." Unlike drugs and alcohol, I would have happily risked expulsion to spend the night with Claire. Unfortunately, between her adenoidal roommate, my insanely attentive housemaster, and the stacks at the Stokes Library being closed for renovation, the opportunity had not presented itself.

I pulled out of the Walgreens parking lot and raced to the nearest public library with the possibilities of expulsion dancing in my head. As happy as I was that Claire had almost finished her essay, part of me was jealous that she had banged it out so quickly. But that was Claire. It didn't matter what the class or assignment, she always put in half the effort and got twice the results. This used to drive me crazy until I'd learned to tolerate it in the same selfless manner I'd learned to tolerate her brains, beauty, and charm.

I fast-talked my way onto an unoccupied computer and clicked on Claire's e-mail, but instead of finding her essay there was an invitation to something called Claire's Christmas Extravaganza.

"Surprise!" she said when I called her back.

"What is this?" I asked.

"Remember when I told you my parents were leaving for Virgin Gorda right after we opened presents on Christmas morning?"

"Yeah."

"I'd planned on spending the week between Christmas and New Year's working on my essay, but now that it's practically finished I decided to throw a party in your honor. I invited all my old friends, and they can't wait to meet you."

"Sounds great, but I'd still like to read your essay."

"Don't worry. You can read it when you get here."

My e-mail pinged, and a message from the Wheaton Financial Aid Office appeared in my in-box. I clicked on the link, and a very real possibility of expulsion appeared on the screen:

Dear Cameron,

It has come to our attention that you failed to disclose a significant amount of income on your financial aid form this year. If there's a reasonable explanation for this oversight, please contact our office immediately. Otherwise, we will be forced to rescind your scholarship for the remainder of the academic year.

Yours truly,
Dean Bell
Director of Financial Aid

I stared at the computer and began to shake. Accepted or not, my admittance to Princeton was contingent on completing my last semester at Wheaton. *A reasonable explanation for this oversight?* Of course there was. Uncle Wonderful knew a guy, who knew a guy, who hacked into Wheaton's computers and did something to my account. And now that I thought about it, he had probably done the same thing to my phone. I stared out the library window and wondered why, out of all the families in the world, I had been born into mine. Was I simply unlucky, or was there something more nefarious at work? Maybe the father I never knew stole a valuable trinket from the gods, and I was doomed to suffer for the rest of my days. It was as good an explanation as any.

Claire asked me a question, and I snapped back to reality.

"What was that?" I replied.

"I said, 'Do you want me to send you the train schedule to Saratoga?' "

"Uh, sure. That would be great."

"Are you all right?" she asked. "Your voice just got all funny."

What I should have said was "Funny? Funny how?" but I was so freaked out by my financial aid fiasco that I accidentally told the truth.

"I'm sorry," I said. "This thing with my mother has me totally freaked out."

"Your mother?" Claire said after a pause. "I thought your mother was dead."

Busted.

I shifted into Weasel Mode and tried to figure out my next move. I hated lying to Claire, and if there was ever a time to tell her the truth about my family this was it. Then I thought about my mother, and Uncle Wonderful, and the hundreds of people I'd robbed, and knew I couldn't tell her. It didn't matter how much she cared about me, Claire was an honest and upright person and would have dumped me before I had even finished my story.

So, I lied. I lied hoping I would never have to lie to her again.

"My mother *is* dead," I said. "Today is the anniversary of her death."

"Oh, Cam, I'm so sorry. You never talk about her."

"I know," I replied truthfully. "It's just too hard."

We finished our conversation, and as I walked out of the library I remembered something Grandpa Patsy told me the day he gave me my good name.

"Remember, Skipper," he said, pulling my passport and birth certificate out of his storage locker, "your good name is the most valuable gift I can ever give you so take very good care of it."

His words still echoed in my ears, and I looked up at the sky and said, "I tried, Grandpa Patsy. I really did."

Then I got in my car and went to kill Uncle Wonderful.

10

TEN MINUTES LATER I PULLED UP TO UNCLE WONDERFUL'S HOUSE ready to pound his nose through the back of his head. After all he'd done for me, it was the least I could do. I barreled up the front walk with my fists squeezed tight and was about to kick down the door when it flew open and Uncle Wonderful appeared holding a gun.

"Hello, Skipper."

"Hi, Uncle Wonderful. Could you do me a favor and put that gun away so I can beat you to death without getting shot?"

"Beat me to death and you won't be going back to that fancy school of yours."

"I'm already not going back to that fancy school of mine, thanks to you."

He held up his hands like a scale. "Uncle Wonderful giveth and Uncle Wonderful taketh away." Then he lowered his arms and said, “Actually, it’s more like the other way around.”

“What are you talking about?”

“I’m saying come inside and maybe, just maybe, we can come to an arrangement that’s beneficial to both of us.”

Seeing no alternative, and not wanting a murder conviction on my permanent record, I unclenched my fists and followed him inside.

“You want a biscotti?” he asked, leading me into the kitchen.

“No, I don’t want a biscotti.”

“Suit yourself.”

He set the gun on the counter and pulled a package of Stella D’oro from the cabinet. As he crumbled two biscotti into a bowl and poured milk over them, I glanced down at his gun and thought about all the times Roy and I had played with it when we were kids. It seemed like every time Uncle Wonderful and Aunt Marie left the house one of us would sneak into their bedroom and get it from the closet shelf. It was a miracle we didn’t shoot each other.

Uncle Wonderful sat down at the kitchen table and mashed up his biscotti with a spoon. “So, here’s the deal,” he began. “We need a second man for a job Roy’s planning and we want that man to be you.”

“No way,” I replied before the last word was out of his mouth.

“But you haven’t heard the terms of the deal yet.”

“It doesn’t matter. I’m out of the game. End of story.”

He sighed then stuck his fingers deep in his mouth and pulled out his teeth. Uncle Wonderful had always been vain about his looks, and the slicked-back hair, golf-pro image he'd been cultivating since I was a kid looked totally ridiculous without teeth.

"Yuck," I said, turning away. "Do you have to do that right at the table?"

He placed the teeth on a saucer and said, "What's the matter? Haven't you ever seen a pair of falsies before?"

"Not on you."

"Get used to them, kiddo, because they're a permanent part of my life from now on."

"What happened to your old ones?"

"Nothing special. I always had lousy teeth, and when I figured out a way to get the Veteran's Administration to pay for them I figured it was time for an upgrade."

"But you're not a veteran," I said.

"A mere detail," Uncle Wonderful said with a smile. "They had to make three sets, the incompetent jerks, but this pair fits like a glove. The only problem is I haven't gotten used to wearing them while eating."

"What did you do with the other two pairs?" I asked.

"I keep them for backup in case something happens to these. Now back to the business at hand." He shoveled a spoonful of mushy biscotti into his mouth and said, "Maybe I didn't explain myself properly a minute ago, so let me say it differently. You help Roy with this job, and I'll make sure that problem with your scholarship goes away."

"What about Vinny? I thought he was Roy's partner."

"Vinny's good people, but this job requires a little more finesse than Vinny's capable of." He picked up his teeth and gun and said, "Think about it for a minute. I gotta wash these things off and apply more adhesive."

"To the dentures or the gun?" I asked with a grin.

"Don't be a wisenheimer."

He walked away, and I looked around the kitchen. Despite the fact that I wanted to murder Uncle Wonderful, I had nothing but fond memories of this house and eating Sunday dinner there with Aunt Marie and Grandpa Patsy. It was one of the few permanent things in my life.

As was my family's nonsense.

I grabbed a biscotti from the package and weighed my options. There were two, as far as I could tell: I could say yes to Uncle Wonderful's offer and go back to school and a life of infinite possibilities. Or I could say no, and . . .

And *what*? Live on the streets? Sleep in a cardboard box?

My choices were limited, and they both stank. I racked my brain trying to think of an alternative, but there wasn't one. I had to take Roy's job, and my only wiggle room was in the details.

Uncle Wonderful reappeared with his teeth back where they were supposed to be and sat down at the table.

"So?" he asked. "What's it gonna be?"

"I'll do it."

"Good."

Then I held up a finger and said, "After I hear about the job."

"It's Roy's deal. He'll fill you in on the details."

"Okay, but just remember. I'm strictly backup on this. I'll drive, do recon, make phone calls. I'll do whatever it takes as long as no one outside the family knows I'm involved."

Uncle Wonderful nodded. "Sounds good to me."

"So what's my cut?"

"Your cut? Your cut is I don't break your arms for stealing Grandpa Patsy's money."

"Grandpa Patsy's money?" I replied with an innocence I'd been rehearsing for the last four years. "I have no idea what you're talking about."

"Save it. We opened Grandpa Patsy's storage locker after the funeral, and it was empty. You were the only one besides me and your mother who knew where it was."

I looked him in the eye. "Did you ask her if she stole it?"

"Of course I did."

"And?"

"She said she didn't."

"And you believed her?" I said with a laugh. "Why?"

"Because you took off."

"I took off because I didn't want to be a thief for the rest of my life. Think about it. Where did the money for Mom's new house come from? And that Mustang out there didn't just buy itself."

A look of confusion crossed his face, and I thought I had

him until he gritted his dentures and said, "Listen up, you little snot. You say one more bad thing about your mother and, job or no job, I'll break your arms."

I held up my hands and said, "Sorry, but I still need to be compensated for the money I would have made working in the cafeteria back at school."

"How much are we talking about here?"

"Let's see, twenty hours a week for two weeks, plus double time on Christmas. With tax and tip that's . . ." I pretended to run the numbers in my head. "Three-hundred-and-fifty dollars."

Uncle Wonderful burst out laughing. "Three-hundred-and-fifty bucks for two weeks' work? You're getting taken."

"It's honest money."

"If you say so. I just never realized honesty came at such a steep discount." He pulled out his wallet and said, "I'll tell you what. Just to show you what a nice guy I am, I'll throw in an extra fifty bucks and make it an even four hundred."

Uncle Wonderful counted out four hundred dollars and handed it to me. I felt a little guilty lying to him—the school cafeteria was closed for the holidays, and I wouldn't have made a dime during the break—but I needed the money to visit Claire. Better still, the cash said Uncle Wonderful believed—at least a tiny bit—that my mother had robbed Grandpa Patsy's storage locker. And the more I thought about it, the more I realized he must have thought that all along.

Otherwise, he would have already broken my arms.

11

THE AMOUNT OF MONEY IN GRANDPA PATSY'S STORAGE locker was always this big family mystery, and estimates ranged everywhere from five hundred thousand dollars all the way up to five million. Imagine my surprise when I broke into it, and there was only a hundred thousand dollars inside. But the more I thought about it, the more sense it made. Growing up, I'd watched Grandpa Patsy throw away hundreds, sometimes thousands of dollars each week betting on football and basketball games. Those kinds of losses add up, and I knew of at least two bookies who had sent their grandkids to Catholic school on Grandpa Patsy's nickel. This last fact weighed heavily on my grandfather and was why, when I showed him a brochure for Wheaton Academy, he offered to pay my way. After a lifetime of betting on losers, he said with a tear in his eye, he wanted to go out backing a winner.

The only problem was Grandpa Patsy died without telling anyone about his promise to me. This was probably a good thing, considering my mother or Uncle Wonderful would have talked him out of it, but it put me in the tricky situation of having to steal money that was rightfully mine. Wheaton cost thirty thousand dollars a year, and my intention was to take only what I needed for four years of school. This plan went up in flames the moment I saw how much money was really inside that locker. My family had been drooling over Grandpa Patsy's fortune for years, and there was no way they'd believe there was only a hundred grand left, and it all belonged to me.

One of Grandpa Patsy's favorite sayings was that money separates friends, and big money separates families. I'm not saying a hundred thousand dollars is small money, but it sure ain't five million bucks, and I knew that no matter what I did, the contents of that locker would tear my family apart. I also knew that if I ran away they'd think I stole more money than I actually had. Any way I looked at it, I was screwed. I stared at the money for a long time and tried to figure out what to do. Yes, I wanted to go to Wheaton, and yes, I wanted to get away from my family, but I was only thirteen years old, and the thought of running away from everything I knew was terrifying. Then I remembered Grandpa Patsy saying he wanted to go out backing a winner and I took the money.

Unfortunately, four years of Wheaton cost more than a hundred thousand dollars. This would not have been a problem for Skip O'Rourke, but Cam Smith was determined to fund his education honestly. Therefore, instead of robbing department stores or dealing drugs, I got a job in the school cafeteria, worked two and three jobs during the summer, and applied for every scholarship I could find. And somehow, even with two tuition hikes and a twenty-five percent increase in fees, I managed to pay for school and get accepted to Princeton. It was the hardest thing I had ever done, and I was incredibly proud of it.

This was why I found myself going to Roy's apartment instead of running away like a sane person.

"What time is it?" Roy asked, answering the door with a yawn.

"Nearly four. Talk about sleeping the day away."

"Can it, half pint. I only got to bed a couple of hours ago."

"Why were you up so late?"

"The job."

"What job?" I asked.

"I'll tell you after I take a shower."

I followed him inside, and the first thing I noticed was an elite racing bike leaning against the wall.

"That's one sweet-looking ride," I said, inspecting the bicycle. "Do you take it out a lot?"

"Not as much as I'd like. Especially considering how much it's worth."

I hopped on the bike and squeezed the hand brakes. "How much does something like this cost?"

"Three G's. And that's just for the frame."

"Wow, that's a lot of money for just two wheels."

"Tell me about it. The guy I stole it from must be majorly pissed. You should get one, too. We can play Crash."

"With three-thousand-dollar bikes?"

"Why not? Life's too short to ride a Schwinn."

Roy disappeared into the bathroom, and I pedaled across the apartment. It took less than a second, and by the time I reached the opposite wall I wanted to steal a bike just like it for myself.

Be careful, a little voice inside me said. *None of this is real.*

I leaned the bike against the wall and tried to remember the last time Roy and I had played Crash. I couldn't, and felt sad because playing Crash was one of the highlights of my childhood. Roy and I invented the game out of boredom, and the rules were easy as one, two, three:

1. Steal a couple of bicycles
2. Chase each other until one of us crashed
3. Repeat until bleeding

Yes, I know it sounds stupid, but Crash was a total blast, and the more we played it, the more fun we had. We added a scoring system to keep things interesting, and points were awarded for the amount of time played, the value of the bike stolen, and the condition of the bike at the end of the game. Points were deducted for falls, blood spilled, and broken bones. Concussions and death ended play, and double-secret bonus points were awarded for causing traffic accidents and getting chased by the cops. No one was ever seriously injured, but I lost half my front tooth and Roy broke his wrist. The absolute high point of the entire escapade was the time we forced a redneck in a Dodge Ram to drive straight into a bread truck. It was awesome. The guy went totally ballistic and chased us all over Copiague, screaming his head off and cursing like a psychopath.

Crash was idiotic for any number of reasons, but it had everything a twelve-year-old boy could ask for including thrills, spills, and the possibility of getting arrested. The next step would have been to swap our bikes for cars, but I ran away before we could graduate to the next level. This was probably a good thing, considering at least one of us would have ended up dead or in jail.

"You ever hear of Fat Nicky Gangliosi?" Roy asked, strolling out of the bathroom with a towel wrapped around his waist.

"Is he the guy you stole that bike from?"

"Not even close." Roy grabbed a jar of Vaseline off the table and slathered it all over a fresh tattoo on his arm. "Twenty years ago Fat Nicky was reigning champion of the New York crime world. Then about ten years ago he got shot up in a botched murder attempt and had to retire. Now his son runs the business, and Fat Nicky sits around all day watching cooking shows. You with me so far?"

"I guess."

"Good, because our job is to kill him."

I waited for Roy to say he was joking, and when he didn't I said, "Are you crazy? We're thieves. We don't kill people."

"The world's changed, Skip. Between the recession and all the new security stuff out there, it's impossible to make a living off welfare checks anymore."

"I thought Vinny just got disability."

"For like three weeks. By the time he's done paying off the doctor and the check cashing service, he'll clear barely three bills."

"So why did he do it?"

"Birds gotta fly. Fish gotta swim," Roy said with a shrug. "But listen, I understand your reluctance to cap this guy and I felt exactly the same way."

"Good."

"That's why we're only going to *pretend* to cap him."

This job was getting more ridiculous by the second.

"And what happens after that?" I asked. "Is someone going to pretend to pay us?"

"No, the money's real."

"That's reassuring," I said with a laugh. "And who wants us to kill this guy?"

"Your mother's roommate. Well, he's not actually her roommate. He's more like her neighbor."

"At Shady Oaks? Now I get it. This guy must think he's the Godfather and you're Spider-Man. Who do I get to be? Luke Skywalker, or Indiana Jones?"

"The guy's not in the crazy part of Shady Oaks. He's in the Williams Pavilion."

"What's that?"

"It's their old age home. Besides, the only thing that matters is that his money is sane. Here, check this out."

Roy handed me some forms on Shady Oaks stationery. There were lots of big numbers scattered about and I said, "I never realized Shady Oaks was so expensive. I guess it's a good thing Mom got all that money from Grandpa Patsy, otherwise she'd never be able to afford this place."

"What money?"

"You know, the *money* money. Where'd you get this paperwork from, anyway?"

"The Shady Oaks financial services office."

"You broke in?"

"No, I used my master key." Roy stood up and said, "You're looking at the new night janitor at the Williams Pavilion. That's why I was asleep when you got here."

"But we went to Shooters last night."

"My shift is from midnight till eight in the morning. After I hooked up with Jackie I had her drop me off at Shady Oaks. And speaking of Jackie, she's got this girlfriend that sounds perfect for Vinny. The only problem is her friend's kind of shy and wants Jackie to spend some quality time with Vinny to see if he's boyfriend material. So, take a bath, my favorite cousin, because tomorrow night the four of us are going out to dinner."

"Why do you want me to tag along?"

"To help Vinny impress Jackie. Face it, you're the closest thing to an impressive person we know. What do you say?"

“I’d love to, but I spent all my money at Shooters last night.”

“Don’t worry about the money. It’s my treat.”

A hot meal in a restaurant sounded way better than cold cuts at my mother’s house. “Sure,” I said. “Why not?”

“Good. Just do me a favor. If Vinny asks about the job, pretend like you have no idea what he’s talking about. Okay?”

“Sure thing,” I said, wishing it were true.

12

ON MY WAY HOME FROM ROY'S APARTMENT I THOUGHT about Claire and why I would let myself get sucked back into the bosom of my family so she and I could be together. The short answer was I loved her. But there was more to it than that. Claire was the first person I loved who didn't try to rob me. I'd dated other girls before her, but it never felt like love. It never felt like anything. Then Claire entered my life and stole my heart, which is pretty ironic considering my background.

We hooked up in the fall of our third year at the annual Leaf Peeper Dance. This was the biggest social event of the fall, complete with elaborate decorations, tons of snacks, and a local band from Albany. The band was terrific, but I saw right away that one of the members of their crew was a weasel. Shifty eyes, fake smile, hands in the pockets of a trench coat he never took off, this guy was straight out of the juvenile delinquent handbook. He tried to act cool, but he was physically incapable of keeping his eyes off the big pile of coats and pocketbooks sitting on the edge of the dance floor. I knew exactly what he was thinking because I was thinking the same thing myself.

Full disclosure: my biggest challenge when I arrived at Wheaton was not robbing the school blind. Old habits die hard, and the place was like a candy store run by blind people. All of the students were rich, nobody locked their doors, and the windows were so feeble you could have jimmied them with a Post-it Note. But I was good. I strolled by unattended laptops in the library, ignored wallets and backpacks, and never so much as borrowed a pencil without asking. I was a model citizen, and the most surprising thing about this was how good it made me feel. I didn't have as much spending money as the other kids, but that was fine. I was acting like a normal human being, and that's all that mattered.

This was why I became so angry when I saw that weasel in the trench coat ripping off my classmates. The smart move would have been to notify security and let them handle it, but I wasn't feeling particularly smart that evening. Or merciful. Besides, it was fun to kick back and watch someone else be the thief for a change. The guy knew the band's set list, and whenever they played a good dance song, he'd take advantage of the crowd's enthusiasm and dip into a few pocketbooks. It was a good scam, and within half an hour his pockets were overflowing with wallets and iPhones. Professionally speaking, it was quite a haul.

The band played a slow song to finish their set, and as couples paired up to dance, the weasel headed for the door. This was always my favorite part of a job. There's something positively electric about those last few seconds when you think you're about to get away with a scam that makes it all worthwhile. It's the criminal equivalent of skydiving.

I followed the guy outside and waited for him to think he was home free. Sure enough, halfway to the parking lot he pulled out a cigarette and stopped to light it. This was my cue. I broke into a sprint and aimed for the center of his back. My timing was perfect, and I slammed into him just as the cigarette touched his lips.

"You third-rate slimebag," I hissed as I dove on top of him and pummeled his face. "You think you can come to *my* school and steal from *my* classmates? Well, guess what? You're wrong."

"What the hell are you doing?" someone behind me shouted. "You're hurting him."

"That's kind of the point," I said, looking up.

And that's how I met Claire.

We'd passed in the halls dozens of times and even had a few friends in common, but this was the first time we actually spoke. Her dress was soaked from dancing, and she'd come outside to cool her feet in the fall grass. Christmas was months away, but for some reason her toenails were painted red and green and this struck me as the most exotic thing in the world. I couldn't take my eyes off of them.

"Look at me when I'm yelling at you," she demanded.

"Your wish is my command," I said, and pulled out my cell phone. "What's your phone number?"

"Excuse me?"

"I said, what's your phone number?"

"What's that got to do with anything?"

"A lot. Trust me."

She gave me her digits, and I punched them into my phone. Two seconds later, a Lady Gaga song blared from the trench coat beneath me.

"Hey," she said. "That's my ringtone."

"Exactly. I saw this lowlife stealing stuff and came out here to stop him."

Claire's eyes grew wide. "Then he must have my charm bracelet, too!"

I held up my cell phone. "What's your charm bracelet's phone number?"

"Not funny. My grandmother gave me that bracelet when I was seven, and it means more to me than anything."

"Yo, slimebag," I said, and slapped the guy on the side of the head. "You come across a charm bracelet on your little crime spree?"

"Eat me."

"I'll take that as a yes." I stuck my hand in the trench coat and pulled out a couple of cell phones, some crumpled bills, and a gold charm bracelet.

"Oh my God!" Claire shouted. She grabbed the bracelet and hugged it to her chest. "I only took it off because I was worried some of the charms might fall off while I was dancing. Last year I lost the little gold horseshoe I got for my eighth birthday and almost had a nervous breakdown." A dark look crossed her face, and she glared at the weasel in the trench coat. "You idiot!" she yelled, and pulled back her leg to kick him in the ass. Lucky for him, he saw it coming and twisted out of the way.

I, however, was not so lucky, and the kick landed square on my wrist.

"Ow!" I screamed.

"Oh no!" she screamed back. "Are you all right?"

Before I could answer, the weasel jumped up and raced toward the parking lot. I tried to stop him, but the best I could do was hang on to his trench coat. He pulled himself free, and the coat came off in my hands.

"Jerk!" Claire shouted, and threw a shoe at him. She was a much better kicker than quarterback, and the shoe landed ten feet short.

"Damn it!" she yelled.

"Don't worry about it," I said. "It's going to be a long time before he tries something like that again. I think I broke his nose."

"You did? Nice!"

Not the kind of response you'd expect from the vice president of the junior class who had never so much as given me a second look. Claire went inside and came back with a cup of ice. She held it against my wrist, and I swear it was the warmest thing to ever touch my skin.

"Does it still hurt?" she asked.

It took me a while to answer because I was too busy staring at Claire's face which was so close to mine I could feel her breath. "Yeah, it does," I finally said. "I better go get it checked out."

"I'm so sorry."

"No biggie. Why don't you take that coat inside and give people their stuff back."

"Right," she said, staring at me for a moment too long. "Good idea."

Then she turned and walked back to the party.

I went to the infirmary and didn't expect to hear from Claire again. I was totally shocked, therefore, when I walked out of the infirmary and found her sitting on the steps.

"What are you doing here?" I asked.

"I wanted to thank you again for saving my charm bracelet. How's your wrist?"

"It's just bruised."

"I'm really sorry."

"How's your foot? I'm surprised you didn't break a toe."

"My foot's fine," she said, standing up. "I guess seven years at Miss DeMarco's ballet school finally paid off."

"She must have been a great teacher because that was some kick."

"She was an excellent teacher. Unfortunately, she also had affairs with half the dads in the school, including mine."

"Ouch."

The chapel bell rang in the distance and Claire said,

"That's curfew. We better get back to the dorms."

"Don't worry about me," I said, and pulled a white piece of paper from my pocket. "I have a pass from the infirmary."

Claire looked at the pass. "There's no time written on it. You could stay out all night if you wanted to."

"Why would I want to stay out all night by myself?"

"Who said anything about staying out by yourself?"

"Won't you get in trouble?"

Claire dismissed my worries with a wave of her hand. "My roommate snores like a freight train on steroids, and the floor monitor doesn't even bother to check our room anymore. As long as Campus Safety doesn't catch us we'll be fine."

"Where do you want to go?"

"The Drowning Pool."

"Just the two of us?" I asked.

"I don't see anyone else around, do you?"

"No."

"Then let's go."

The Drowning Pool was a swimming hole behind campus. Rumor had it that a freshman had died there in the nineteen fifties, and a trip to the Drowning Pool was as much a Wheaton right-of-passage as Mrs. Zelinski's first year Latin class.

I followed Claire into the woods, and we were immediately swallowed up by shadows. Leaves and spiderwebs tickled our faces, and the trees and bushes seemed closer than they had just moments before. We followed a trail of pine needles and dappled moonlight until the trees parted and we came to a small lake. Tiny clouds floated over the surface of the water, and I half expected to see a glowing fairy or a chain saw–wielding psychopath flitting about. We found a log by the edge of the water and sat down to take it all in. Claire removed her shoes and as she slipped her feet into the water asked, "What about you?"

"What about me?"

"I showed you mine, now you show me yours."

"Excuse me?"

"I told you about my father and Miss DeMarco. What's your family's deep, dark secret?"

My family has nothing but *deep, dark secrets,* I wanted to reply. Instead I said, "I don't have a family."

"What do you mean? Everybody has a family."

"My parents died when I was a kid, and I got passed around by relatives until I came here."

"That's terrible."

"I don't know, I kind of like it here."

"Not that part, the before-you-came-here part."

"I guess," I said with a shrug. "It was a long time ago, and I really don't like to talk about it."

The lie rolled off my tongue like it always did, except this time it left a strange taste in my mouth. I turned to Claire, and as our eyes met I felt a strange desire to—*Was it, tell the truth*? This made no sense. Yes, I had run away to Wheaton to become an honest person, but that didn't mean

I wanted to stand up in the middle of the dining hall and tell the world my life story.

"I'm so sorry about your family," she said.

"It was a long time ago."

We talked through the night with the chapel bell reminding us—every hour on the hour—of how long we'd been together and how little time we had left. Finally, when the bell struck seven I said, "Ugh, I have to be at work in, like, twenty minutes."

"You have to go to work *this morning*? For how long?"

"Just three hours."

"If I had known that I wouldn't have kept you out all night."

"Are you kidding? I wouldn't have traded this night for all the breakfast shifts in China."

We walked back to campus, and with each step it felt like I was being pulled from a dream and dropped back into reality.

Plus, I still hadn't kissed Claire.

I had wanted to kiss her from the moment our eyes met on the infirmary steps, but I didn't want to appear overly aggressive or presumptuous. Worse than that, I didn't want to try and kiss Claire and have her turn away. That would have been a nightmare. But Claire *had* spent the night with me, and that had to mean something, right? And what if she wanted me to kiss her, and I didn't? Would she think I wasn't interested in her? Or that I was dating someone else? Or that I was gay?

Damn, I thought. *I've had an easier time breaking into apartments than this.*

We reached the edge of the woods, and I could see the chapel spire looming ahead of us. If I didn't kiss Claire now, I told myself, I might not ever have the opportunity again.

"Hey, you," I said, walking up beside her.

"Yes?"

"I just wanted to . . ."

"What?"

"This," I said, and kissed her.

I kept waiting for her to pull away, or kick me in the crotch, or scream, but she didn't do any of those things, so I raised my hand and touched her cheek with the back of my fingers. I know you're not supposed to open your eyes during moments like this, but I couldn't help myself. Not surprisingly, Claire was even more beautiful up close. Her cheeks, her eyebrows, even her earlobes were glorious.

Then the kiss was over, and Claire stepped back to look at me. She had this huge smile on her face and for a split second I was terrified she was going to start laughing. Instead she turned around and said, "See you around, Cam Smith."

"See you around," I replied

Claire walked away, and I stood there feeling both with her and alone.

See you around, Cam Smith.

What did she mean by that? I wondered. *Was she brushing me off? Or did she really want to see me again?*

I was too nervous, and tired, and exhilarated to tell. So I raced to the cafeteria and took my place on the serving line with the memory of Claire's kiss still claiming possession of my lips.

They say breakfast is the most important meal of the day, but it was my least favorite shift to work. Not only did you have to get there super early, but the food was boring and almost everyone there was grumpy. It was even worse after my night with Claire. My wrist throbbed like crazy, and I was so tired from lack of sleep that I almost passed out at the steam table. Lucky for me there were only two choices on the menu which gave me a fifty percent chance of getting it right.

"Oatmeal or eggs?" I mumbled over and over again. "Oatmeal or eggs?"

"Hi, Cam."

I looked up and Claire was standing in front of me. She had changed her clothes, her hair was wet, and she looked even more beautiful than the night before.

"Hey."

"Which of these mouthwatering selections do you recommend?"

"That's a tough one. The oatmeal is bad, and the eggs are even worse. On the bright side, no one's died of food poisoning yet."

"When you put it that way, I think I'll try the oatmeal."

"An excellent choice." I spooned some mush into her

bowl and said, “How are you feeling, by the way?”

“Good. Tired. But good.” She smiled to let me know that she meant it.

“Me too.”

“Want to go to Cassidy’s for lunch when you’re done?” she asked.

Cassidy’s was a diner in town where all the cool kids went to eat. If Claire took me there, it was the equivalent of a front page headline in the *Weekly Wheatonian* announcing we were a couple.

“Absolutely,” I said.

“Great, I’ll swing by your room at eleven.”

Claire walked away, and I exhaled.

See you around, Cam Smith.

So Claire did want to see me again! I was stunned. Claire dated upper classmen, and I was just this little mouse who scurried around the edges of campus. But not only did Claire want to see me again, she wanted to do it in public. This was major. As I stood there slinging oatmeal and eggs I thought about our night together and how, for the first time in forever, I hadn’t been worried about my family, my grades, or even my future. No, none of that mattered because being with Claire made me feel like an actual human being instead of someone who was only pretending to be.

Maybe I wasn’t a little mouse after all.

13

"SEE HIM?" MY MOTHER ASKED, POINTING TO A SKINNY kid walking beside an old woman in a black dress.

"Yes?"

"That's Tony. He's been here three times for drug addiction. The first time he was only thirteen years old. That woman he's with is his grandmother. She's a saint."

I stared at the guy. He seemed normal except, like every patient there, he moved with what I had begun calling the "Shady Oaks Shuffle."

"Do they have a lot of that here?" I asked, attempting to bring up the pharmacy in my mother's medicine cabinet. "Drug addicts, I mean?"

"The Shady Oaks Rehab clinic is one of the best in the state and has had lots of famous patients."

"They told you this?"

"No, but you hear things."

We were sitting in a white wooden gazebo about a hundred yards from the O'Neil Pavilion. There was a cool breeze in the air, a picturesque sunset over my shoulder, and a dog barking in the distance. It was a perfect winter's day, and I had a hard time reconciling the beautiful surroundings with the not-so-beautiful fact that I'd been dragged back into O'Rourkes' World of Crime. I closed my eyes and wondered how long it would be before I was hijacking beer trucks and stealing lumber from construction sites.

"Did Wonderful talk to you about the job?"

I opened my eyes and said, "You know about it?"

"Of course I do. It was my idea."

I bit my lip and sighed. Was there anyone in my family who wasn't involved in this clown show?

"What do you think?" she asked.

"I'm not sure yet. So far, I've only heard the broad strokes."

"Which are?"

"That we're scamming some old guy who wants us to kill an ex-mobster for him."

"That's it in a nutshell. Just remember not to say anything stupid when you meet the mark."

"No way," I said, shooting to my feet. "I already told Uncle Wonderful that I'm strictly backup on this deal. I'm not meeting anybody outside the family, especially not the mark."

"That's going to be a little tricky," she said in a low voice.

"Why?"

"Because here he comes."

I turned and saw an old man in a velour tracksuit hobbling toward us on a pair of wooden canes. He looked harmless enough, although harmless people rarely ask you to kill a guy for them.

"Do you mind if I use the other bench?" he asked when he reached the bottom step of the gazebo.

"Of course not," my mother said. "Sal, this is my son, Skip."

"Visiting from college?" he asked.

"Prep school, actually."

"That's a lot better than me. I never made it past the fifth grade." He climbed onto the gazebo and stuck out his hand. "Sal DeNunsio."

"Skip O'Rourke." We shook, and I noticed that the knuckles on his hand were covered with scars. Nasty ones.

"Sal's a friend of mine from years ago," my mother said. "I almost had a heart attack when I found out he was living at the Williams Pavilion."

"The Williams Pavilion?" I asked, already knowing the answer. "What's that?"

"The hospital's geriatric residence," my mother said.

"That's right," he said with a laugh. "I'm not crazy, just old."

"You seem in pretty good shape to me," I said.

"You ever heard of a fighter having a glass jaw?"

"Sure."

"I got two glass hips. After the second one went, I sold my place and moved here."

"I'm sorry."

"Smartest thing I ever did," he said. "But hey, you folks were talking, and I interrupted. I'll just sit here quietly and read my *Racing Form*."

"Got any hot tips?" I asked.

"Yeah, study hard and go to college."

"I mean with the horses," I said with a laugh.

He unfolded the paper and put on a pair of reading glasses. "Right now I'm trying to choose between Sandy's Pride and Road Runner in the fifth at Aqueduct. What do you think?"

"I don't know much about horses, but the Road Runner always beat the Coyote on television."

Mr. DeNunsio pulled a pencil from behind his ear and scribbled something in the paper. "Then Road Runner it is."

In the distance a couple of orderlies were starting to wheel the older patients inside and I said, "It's almost time to go."

"You're leaving?" my mother asked, snapping back to reality. "Why? When will you be back?"

I heard the panic in her voice and took her hand. "It's okay, Ma. It's just that visiting hours are almost over. I'll be back again in the morning."

"Whew, I thought you meant you were going back to school."

"No, I'll be here through New Year's."

"Good, you had me scared there for a second."

It was upsetting to see my mother acting so fragile. She had always been the tough one in the family, and it was her example that gave me the strength to run away in the first place. As much as I wanted to get back to Wheaton and Claire, a small part of me felt an obligation to stay on Long Island and help my mother get well. *If* she was actually sick, that is. I couldn't tell, and between all my guilt and skepticism I thought my head was going to spin right off my shoulders.

On the drive home the thought of robbing Mr. DeNunsio began to gnaw at me. This wasn't going to be like ripping off a department store, or scamming some faceless bureaucracy. Mr. DeNunsio was a real human being with thoughts, hopes, and desires, and how would I have liked it if a couple of knuckleheads stole my life's savings? Granted, I would have never asked a couple of knuckleheads to kill a man for me, but I'm sure Mr. DeNunsio had his reasons. Either way, the job stank and I wanted to get as far away from it as possible.

Think, I told myself. There has to be some way to get out of this thing. Uncle Wonderful might have had connections at the Wheaton financial aid office, but he wasn't God.

Then it hit me: my car. The Mustang was registered in my name—or at least one of them—and if I sold it, the proceeds would not only make up for my scholarship, but give me a head start on Princeton. My desperation vanished, and I drove to the nearest Ford dealership where I was delighted to see that a new GT cost over thirty thousand dollars. Considering there were less than two hundred miles on mine, I could easily clear twenty grand on the deal. Life was looking up.

Or was it?

That car was a gift from your mother, I reminded myself. A big one, too. And if ripping off Mr. DeNunsio was cruel and heartless, selling my Mustang while my mother was possibly suicidal was not only cruel and heartless, but karmically bankrupt.

Except I didn't believe in karma. I believed in working hard and doing the exact opposite of everything I was taught growing up. And that's exactly what selling my Mustang would allow me to do. It might not have been the gift my mother had intended, but it was the best thing she could have done for me—whether she liked it or not.

I was exhausted from spending the previous night on the bathroom floor, but when I got home I couldn't sleep. All I could think about was going back to school and escaping my family permanently. The only hitch in this plan was whether the Mustang was paid for or not, and before I knew what I was doing I was tearing the house apart searching for the title.

My first stops were to my mother's usual hiding places: under the sink, on top of the refrigerator, and in the empty mayonnaise jar in the pantry. I found nothing. Either she had gotten more ingenious in her old age, or she had nothing to hide—both of which I found impossible to believe. Next, I checked all her secondary spots: inside the toilet tank, under the rugs, and behind the dresser in the bedroom. Still nothing. I was about to call it a night when I spotted a piece of loose molding beneath her nightstand. I pulled it free, and in a spot where the Sheetrock didn't quite meet the floor, I spied some metal that looked like the bottom of a document box. Bingo. As I reached down to pull away the Sheetrock my weasel senses began to tingle, and it occurred to me that the plaster work was much better than my mother could have done on her own. This meant someone else knew about the box, and that I should probably cover my tracks.

I went into the kitchen and came back with a steak knife. A matte knife would have been better, but I took my time and cut around the Sheetrock until it pulled free and the box tumbled to the floor. There was nothing special about the box except that it was locked, and I didn't have the key. I could have wasted more time searching for it, but I figured the odds of me finding the key were slim to nothing. At this point your average weasel would have put the box back and hired a guy to make a fake title. Except I wasn't your average weasel; I was an O'Rourke. Something in that box was important, and I needed to find out what it was.

I picked up the box and threw it on the floor. Nothing happened. I tried again and got the same results. By my sixth attempt, I should have accepted that this was not the best way to open a sealed document box, but I was tired, cranky, and growing more frustrated by the second. I threw the box down one last time and, for lack of a better idea, carried it to the garage and wedged it under a rear tire of my Mustang. I cranked the engine and backed up until I heard a pop. Success. I pried open the box and found a passport, birth certificate, and driver's license all made out to someone named Dolores Spencer. I had never met Dolores Spencer, but she bore an uncanny resemblance to my mother.

Why? Because Dolores Spencer was my mother's good name. She had never told me this, of course, but the paperwork said it all. It was something else, too—leverage. I hoped it would never come to it, but if my family made a move against me I now had a bargaining chip. I turned the box upside down and a shower of wallet candy fell to the floor. In addition to the license and passport, there were credit cards, a Social Security card, and membership cards for AAA and AARP. All were slightly worn and all were up to date. It was the best fake identity I had ever seen, and I was impressed by my mother's thoroughness.

"If only you could use your powers for good," I said aloud.

I thumbed through the rest of the paperwork, but the title for the Mustang wasn't there. On to Plan B and finding someone who could print up a bogus title. As I put the paperwork back in the box I spotted the date on Dolores Spencer's driver's license. It was three months old—as was her AAA card and both her credit cards. This made absolutely no sense. Why? Because a person who applies for an AAA card isn't thinking about killing herself. Not in a million years.

A person who applies for an AAA card is thinking about *going* somewhere.

14

THE PLAN WAS TO MEET AT THE OLIVE GARDEN AT EIGHT o'clock. I picked up Vinny at seven thirty and got there ten minutes early. Roy picked up Jackie and got there twenty minutes late. This gave Vinny and me half an hour to watch as every bar stool, table, and drink coaster in the restaurant got taken. By the time Roy and Jackie arrived there was a twenty minute wait, and I was so hungry my stomach was starting to digest itself.

"This place is jammed," I said. "Let's go across the street to the Sizzler."

"No way," Vinny said. "I've been looking forward to a Never Ending Pasta Bowl all day."

I turned to Roy and Jackie, but they were too busy making out to offer an opinion. I pulled out my phone and checked the time.

"This is ridiculous," I said. "We've been waiting almost

forty minutes." I tapped Roy on the shoulder. "Hey, we need to talk."

Roy untangled his tongue from Jackie's tonsils and said, "What's up?"

"You want to get going?"

"But we've only been here like a couple of minutes."

"No. *You've* only been here like a couple of minutes. Vinny and I have been here since Washington crossed the Delaware. C'mon, let's go to the Sizzler."

"But they don't give you all the pasta you can eat."

"Who cares? I'm ready to eat my sneakers at this point."

Roy sighed. "All right. Let me go talk to the hostess." He turned to Jackie. "You want to come?"

"Sure. You boys want anything from the bar?"

"Absolutely," Vinny replied. "Get me a Heineken."

"What about you, Skip?"

My hangover was still fresh in my mind and I said, "I'll have a Sprite."

"You sure you don't want something harder? Like a glass of milk?" Jackie asked.

"No, Sprite's fine."

"Suit yourself."

The happy couple headed for the bar, and Vinny stood up and cracked his neck. "Wanna go outside and fire up a joint?"

"No thanks. I didn't sleep very well last night, and if I smoke anything now I'll pass out in my Never Ending Pasta Bowl."

"Okay, tell Roy I'm around the corner."

Vinny stepped outside, and when I checked my phone I was delighted to see that another minute had passed. The way things were going we'd be eating dinner sometime in the next century.

Roy reappeared a few minutes later looking triumphant. "I slipped the hostess a ten spot and the next available table is ours."

"Fabulous."

"Where's Vinny?"

"Getting high."

"Excellent," he said, and turned toward the door.

"What about Jackie?" I asked.

"She's talking to the bartender. When she gets back tell her that me and the Vinster are outside."

Four never-ending minutes later Jackie appeared with our drinks.

"Here," she said, handing me a glass filled with a pale yellow liquid.

"What's this?" I asked.

"A white wine spritzer. I know you wanted a Sprite and everything, but it's two-for-one night, and I didn't want to waste a free drink on just soda."

I took a sip and said, "It tastes pretty good. Thanks."

"No problem. Where's Roy?"

"Out getting stoned with Vinny. If you want to join them I can stay here and listen for our names."

"No, thanks. Pot makes me sleepy."

"I know what you mean."

I took another sip of my drink. Roy had said it was my job to impress Jackie, but I couldn't think of anything impressive to say. The best I could do was compliment Jackie on her dancing, which I was about to do when she looked down at me and said, "You treat Roy like crap."

"Excuse me?" I sputtered.

"He told me that you were like his oldest friend in the world, but I don't buy it. Wanna know what I see?"

"Uh, what?"

"I see a guy who goes off to some fancy school and comes back thinking his shit don't smell."

I didn't know what Roy had told Jackie about me and said, "I'm sorry. My mom's been sick."

"Big deal. My father dropped dead of a heart attack, and I still talked to my friends."

I was at a loss for words. Jackie may have been obnoxious, but maybe she did have a point. "I'm sorry," I finally said. "But if it's any consolation, last time I went to the toilet it sure didn't smell like potpourri."

Jackie ignored my lame attempt at humor and said, "You think you're so different from Roy and Vinny, but let me tell you something. You're just like them. The way you talk. The way you act. It's i-freaking-dentical."

She took a sip of her drink, and I noticed a small scar above her left eye. I was about to ask her about it when she leaned in and said, "This waitress I know got this hotshot Wall Street trader to put her up in a nice apartment. Now whenever I run into her she acts like she doesn't know me. But let me tell you something. The girl's a joke. She thinks she's so high and mighty in her five-hundred-dollar heels and Michael Kors dresses, but she's still a Shooters' Girl and everyone knows it but her. I can't wait until the guy dumps her so I can laugh in her face."

I stared at Jackie and sighed. Talk about the night from hell. Not only was I exhausted and starving, but now I was getting chewed out by someone I'd known less than five minutes. I didn't think things could get any worse when the door flew open and Vinny burst in.

"Yo, Skip, get out here quick. They're tugging your ride."

"What?"

"Your car! Some dudes are jacking it."

I raced outside and saw two men hooking up my Mustang to a tow truck.

"Hey," I shouted. "What the hell are you doing?"

A big guy with a shaved head and handlebar mustache looked up from the bumper. "You Stephen O'Rourke?" he asked.

I was so upset it took me a moment to remember that Stephen O'Rourke was the name I was using at that particular moment.

"Yeah," I said. "What about it?"

The guy held out a greasy hand. "Keys."

"I'm not giving you my keys."

"Fine, then any damage we do to the vehicle is added to the lien."

"What lien? What the hell are you talking about?"

He jammed a piece of pink paper in my face. "This is a sheriff's order authorizing me to take possession of this car for delinquency of payments."

"What does that mean?"

"It means pay your bills, Johnny Appleseed. Now hand over the keys, or I swear we'll mess up this vehicle so bad your credit rating will be trashed for the rest of your life."

I turned to Roy for help.

"Give the man your keys, Skip."

Seeing no alternative, I did as I was told. I held out my keys, and as the guy reached for them, I pushed the panic button on the fob. The car alarm blared, and the second repo man fell backward and landed flat on his butt.

"Sorry about that," I said with a shrug. "My bad."

The repo men went back to work and, if nothing else, I now knew who my car belonged to: the finance company. Vinny fired up a sympathy joint, and he and Roy passed it back and forth as we watched them tow my car away. At least the repo guys kept their word and didn't trash it in front of me.

"Hey, Roy!" Jackie called from the restaurant. "Our table is ready."

"Excellent," Roy and Vinny replied simultaneously.

With nothing better to do, I trudged back to the Olive Garden. Not only had I just kissed my ride to Claire's good-bye, I'd also bid adieu to my only chance of escaping my family. I glanced over at Roy who was so high he was practically levitating and wondered if what Jackie said was true. Was I just like him? Sure, we talked alike, and sometimes we even dressed alike, but so what? That didn't make us the same person. I had a 3.92 GPA at one of the most prestigious prep schools in the country. I had ambition to be something more than just a successful criminal. Those things had to count for something. Then again, how long would my gold-plated ambition last if returned to Long Island permanently?

Use your head, I told myself. There has to be some way to untangle yourself from this mess. Some kind of double cross . . .

And isn't that exactly what an O'Rourke would think? a voice inside me replied.

It was, and I felt like screaming. No matter what I did, no matter how hard I tried, my inner weasel always reigned supreme. Who was I trying to kid? Didn't I lie to get into Wheaton in the first place? And Princeton, too? Wasn't I lying every time I failed to tell Claire who I really was?

Why even bother asking that question? I said to myself. *Every cell in your body is tattooed with the DNA of a weasel. Face the facts, you were born a thief and you'll die a thief. Why not just accept your fate and get on with your life?*

I hated to admit it, but sometimes I wished that I had never heard of Wheaton Preparatory Academy. True, I never would have met Claire and got accepted to Princeton, but I wouldn't have known any better. I'd be the prize crook in a family of crooks. The pick of the litter. And maybe, just maybe, I'd be happy instead of desperate and overwhelmed, which was how I felt at that moment.

But hey, there was a Never Ending Pasta Bowl in my future, so at least I had that going for me. The hostess led us to our table, and as we sat down Jackie turned to me and asked, "Did those guys really just repossess your car?"

"Yeah," I replied.

"Wow," she said with just the hint of a smile. "That really sucks for you."

15

IT TOOK TWO BUSES PLUS A TWENTY-MINUTE WALK TO GET to Shady Oaks the next morning, and by the time I arrived I was as depressed as I had ever been in my life. I know it sounds crazy, but even after Uncle Wonderful kidnapped me, and my cell phone went dead, and I read the e-mail obliterating my scholarship, I still thought I could somehow beat my family at their own game. But as I rode the N81 along Sunrise Highway and watched the parade of unhappy souls trudge on and off, I knew the O'Rourkes had won. No matter how I looked at it, I was back to being a thief.

"That son of a bitch!" my mother yelled when I told her about my car getting towed.

"Who?" I asked.

"Who do you think? My no good, lousy brother."

"I don't understand."

"He was supposed to keep up the payments until I got out of here. I gave him power of attorney and everything."

"You signed over power of attorney to Uncle Wonderful?" I said with a laugh. "No wonder you're in Shady Oaks."

"Save it, and hand me your phone."

I did as my mother asked, and as she put my temporary cell phone to her ear I leaned in a little closer to make sure she was talking to a real person and not just faking the conversation.

"Wonderful?" she shouted into the phone. "What's this I hear about Sonny's car being clipped? I don't know what you're trying to pull here, but it's stopping right now. You hear me? What?" A look of concern crossed her face. "Really? It costs that much a week? Couldn't you have found someplace cheaper?" She listened for a moment and said, "No, no, I'm sure you did the right thing."

It was an excellent performance, and I couldn't tell if she was lying or not. Not that it mattered because I knew I would never see that Mustang again.

"I'm sorry," she said, handing me the phone. "Wonderful used your car money to pay for this place. You wouldn't believe how expensive it is."

"Doesn't your insurance pay for it?"

"Yes and no. We tried to pull a Medicaid scam—which was why we used my real name in the first place—but it doesn't cover half as much as we thought. The way things are going, I might even lose the house."

"I'm sorry, Ma."

She looked down at the floor and sighed. "I'm the one who should be sorry. The house and car were for you. It all was."

"I know and I really appreciate it," I said, taking her hand. "It's not your fault Uncle Wonderful got to Grandpa Patsy's storage locker first."

I could feel her grip on my hand tighten ever so slightly and she asked, "What are you talking about?"

"Grandpa Patsy's money. I just assumed Uncle Wonderful took it. I mean, otherwise paying for this place wouldn't be a problem, right?"

"Riiiiiiiight."

The best thing about lying to a liar is watching their face as they try to measure the angles. Maybe my mother wasn't 100 percent certain that I'd taken the money, but she *was* 100 percent certain that Uncle Wonderful would have taken it given the opportunity. She put an unlit cigarette in the corner of her mouth and said, "Then I guess it's a good thing I ran into Sal DeNunsio. He could be the answer to all of our problems."

Nice comeback, I wanted to reply. Instead I said, "Yeah, talk about winning the Irish Sweepstakes."

We put on our coats and went outside to hit the gazebo. The sun, the breeze, and the barking dog were still there, but they now felt as inviting as the view from a jail cell. I tried to keep a smile on my face and was doing a pretty good job of it when Roy appeared.

"Hello, Royston," my mother said. "What brings you to Shady Oaks so early?"

Roy handed her a bag of M&M's and said, "Somebody's gotta give this car-less loser a ride home."

"You always were a good boy."

"Thanks, Aunt Sheila."

We dropped off my mother at the O'Neil Pavilion, and I followed Roy to the employees' parking lot.

"What's up?" I asked as we climbed into his Lexus. "Something tells me you didn't come here to give me a ride home."

"Of course not. We have to plan the job."

"Oh goody. I've been wondering how we're going to pull off this magic trick without Mr. DeNunsio finding out Fat Nicky is still alive."

"That's the beauty of it," Roy replied. "DeNunsio wants this done on the down low. Part of the deal is that we're supposed to make the body disappear after we cap him."

I held up my hand like a traffic cop. "Wait a minute. You just said *we*? Mr. DeNunsio doesn't know I'm involved in this, right?"

"That would be correct."

"Good, because like I told your dad, I don't want anyone outside the family knowing I'm part of this thing. One word gets out, and I'm gone. You understand?"

"I wouldn't have it any other way."

"Good."

I didn't believe Roy for a second, but at least I'd drawn a

line in the sand. If someone in my family crossed it, I now had the perfect excuse to quit the job and flush my life down the toilet forever.

"Just out of curiosity," I asked. "With no body and no pictures in the paper, how do we prove we killed Fat Nicky? Or is Mr. DeNunsio just going to take our word for it?"

"Of course not. He wants a scalp."

"He wants us to scalp the guy? How do we do that without killing him?"

"No, doofus. A scalp is something that absolutely, positively belongs to the victim. In this case, DeNunsio wants a picture."

"What kind of picture?"

"An autographed picture of Frank Sinatra."

"The singer?"

"Old Blue Eyes himself. Sinatra was like a god to these guys. They practically worshipped at his feet."

"That doesn't sound very hard," I said. "There must be a million pictures of Frank Sinatra on the Internet. Let's just print one out and autograph it ourselves."

"Not so fast. The picture DeNunsio wants is a Polaroid of Fat Nicky and Frank Sinatra taken backstage at Caesars Palace. It's Fat Nicky's most prized possession, and there's only one like it in the world."

"That makes things a bit more challenging."

"Only a little. But don't worry, I've got it all figured out. Fat Nicky has a hard time breathing from all the lead in his chest, and twice a month he gets these big oxygen tanks delivered. I slipped the guy who drops them off fifty bucks, and he told me the picture of Frank Sinatra is hanging above the TV in the living room. It's the perfect setup. All we need is a van, some uniforms, and a couple of oxygen tanks. That way we can pretend to work for the oxygen company and steal the picture when Fat Nicky isn't looking."

I thought about it a second and said, "That's the dumbest plan I've ever heard."

"Why?" Roy replied, looking hurt. "What's the matter with it?"

I held up a finger. "One, uniform or no uniform, Fat Nicky isn't letting a total stranger into his house. The first thing he's going to do is call the oxygen company and—boom—we're busted. Two, let's say we do get lucky and steal that picture. All roads still lead back to the oxygen company, and do you really think your guy will keep quiet if Fat Nicky puts a gun to his head? And three, there's no way I'm letting Fat Nicky see my face. Sorry, cuz, your plan stinks."

"Fine. You got a better one?"

I thought about it for a minute and said, "Why don't we just break into Fat Nicky's house and steal the picture while he's asleep."

"You can do that?"

"Not me. *You*."

"No way."

"Why not? You've broken into a thousand houses. Why should Fat Nicky's be any different?"

"Because the guy's a mobster."

"I thought you said he was retired. And besides, he's hooked up to an oxygen tank. How dangerous could he be?"

Roy chewed on a thumbnail. "You know," he said after a minute. "You might be on to something here."

16

THE ONLY GOOD THING ABOUT TAKING ROY'S JOB WAS THAT my old cell phone started working again. I'm not saying Uncle Wonderful had anything to do with it, I'm just saying that the person responsible for it was probably named Uncle Wonderful.

"Hello," I croaked a couple of mornings later when the phone in question rang and woke me from a sound sleep.

"Yo, Skip. It's Vinny."

"What's up?"

"Bad news, man."

"What?"

"Roy was in a wreck last night."

I sat up in bed and tried to force myself into something resembling consciousness. "Is he all right?"

"He got thrown from the car and both his legs are broken, but that's not the worst of it. Jackie was killed."

"What?"

"Jackie's dead. They were driving back from the Shooters in Quogue, and Roy hit an ice patch."

"Holy shit. We just saw her the other night."

"I know. It just doesn't seem real. It's like—I don't know—something out of a nightmare. Roy just got out of the emergency room, and they're taking him to his parents' house. I'm going over there now. You want me to pick you up on the way?"

"Absolutely."

Vinny hung up, and I stared at the pile of dirty laundry on the chair in front of me. Jackie dead? How was that possible? She was just telling me what an asshole I was. I climbed out of bed and stumbled into the bathroom.

Can life really be that random? I wondered as I splashed some water on my face. After all, if Vinny hadn't gotten his disability check on the day Uncle Wonderful kidnapped me, Jackie wouldn't have met Roy, and she'd still be alive. Was that all it took? The chance approval of a forged form? I felt sick to my stomach and sat down. Grandpa Patsy was the only other person I knew who had died, but he was old and drank like a fish. At least that made sense. But Jackie was young. She was vibrant. She was a bitch. It seemed terrible and wrong in a thousand different ways, and I kept hoping Vinny would call me back and say it was a joke.

But it wasn't a joke, and as we drove to Uncle Wonderful's house I couldn't shake the feeling that Jackie's death was partially my fault. That by accepting Roy's offer I had somehow opened a Pandora's box of bad luck. Deep down, some part of me hoped Roy was just scamming us and that this was part of some elaborate con and Jackie was still alive. But that hope evaporated the moment we pulled up to Uncle Wonderful's house and saw a sheriff's car parked in the driveway.

"What's that all about?" I asked.

"Roy was DWI."

"Damn."

"Tell me about it. Roy was too banged up to be arraigned, so he has to wear a monitor on his ankle until he can appear in court. There was also a little problem with his car."

"What kind of problem?"

"It was accidentally stolen."

"How can a car be accidentally stolen?"

"He accidentally forgot to scratch the VIN number off one of the windows."

"That'll do it."

We got out of Vinny's car, and as we walked up to the house a fat sheriff stepped out and blocked the path to the door. "Can I help you gentlemen?" he asked.

"We're with the bride's family," I said.

He held out his hand. "Let's see some ID."

We gave him our licenses, and he stared at them at least five times longer than necessary. When he was finally through he handed them back and said, "Enjoy the ceremony, smart ass."

We walked inside and found Roy lying in a hospital bed in the living room. There was an IV in his arm, and his legs were suspended from a metal contraption attached to the bed. Aunt Marie was slouched in a chair next to him and jumped up when she saw me.

"Skip," she said, wrapping her arms around my chest. "I was so sorry to hear about your poor mother."

I tried to reply, but the combination of Aunt Marie's bone-crushing hug and industrial-strength perfume made speaking impossible. Not that this was anything new. Aunt Marie had been shattering my vertebrae for as long as I could remember. She was black Irish—which was our way of saying Italian—and everything about her was big: her hair, her hugs, and especially the trays of ziti she cooked every Sunday. When she was finished dislocating my spine, she took a step back and gave me the once-over.

"Look at you, Skip. You're all grown up."

"Getting older will do that to a guy."

"Not every guy," Uncle Wonderful said, and punched Roy's arm. "Some guys get older, and they still act like they're five years old."

"Be careful," Roy whined. "You break that IV, and the needle could go straight to my heart and kill me."

"We should only be so lucky." Uncle Wonderful grunted and punched him even harder.

"So, how's it going?" Vinny asked, trying to lighten the mood.

"Not too bad," Roy said. "And after meeting so many

amazing doctors and technicians I'm seriously considering a career in the medical arts. Did you know it takes only two years to become a licensed respiratory specialist?"

Roy's drugged-out blabbering was more than Aunt Marie could take, and she grabbed her purse off the floor. "C'mon, Wonderful. If we don't get to the pork store by ten thirty, they run out of the sausage with the broccoli rabe you like."

Roy perked up. "You guys going to the pork store? Can you bring me back some soppressata?"

"You want soppressata?" Marie shouted, stomping out of the room. "After what you did to that poor girl you can eat Oscar Mayer for all I care."

When she was gone, Uncle Wonderful turned to Roy and asked, "You want the sweet soppressata, or the hot?"

"Both."

"I'll see what I can do."

"And some Peroni if they got it."

Uncle Wonderful sighed. "Do you really think drinking beer is a good idea right now?"

"Why? It's not like I can go anywhere."

I followed Uncle Wonderful outside and said, "What the hell was that stunt with my Mustang?"

The sheriff was still parked in the driveway, and Uncle Wonderful nodded toward the side of the house. "Step into my office." I followed him behind a pine tree, and he jammed a finger in my chest. "First off," he hissed, "I'm getting a little tired of your attitude. I run this family now, and you better start showing me a little respect."

"Grandpa Patsy never asked for special treatment."

"I'm not Grandpa Patsy."

"You can say that again."

"And second, there's been a little change with the job."

"Of course there has. It's off."

"The hell it is. It's your job now. You start Monday night at the Williams Pavilion."

I wrapped my hand around his finger, and it took all my self-control not to bend it backward until it snapped. "First off," I said, "even if I was doing this job—which I'm not—why would I want to work at the Williams Pavilion?"

"Because Sal DeNunsio wants to walk you through the particulars of the deal himself."

"You told him I was involved?"

"Of course I did. It was the only way I could keep this thing from falling apart."

I let go of his finger and bunched my hands into fists. "I told you, nobody outside the family was supposed to know I'm involved."

"Things changed."

"You're damn right things changed, because I'm out and I don't care what you do. You can turn off my phone, you can mess with my financial aid, and you can wipe your shoes all over my good name. I don't care anymore. You're a piece of garbage, Uncle Wonderful, and you always have been."

"You ungrateful little—"

The rest of his words were cut off when he took a swing

at me. I dodged the punch, but I didn't see the knife in his other hand until it was too late. He aimed it straight at my solar plexus and backed me against the house.

"You know something," I said in the calmest voice I could muster. "In ten years of scamming people no one has ever pointed a weapon at me. Not once. And since I've been home you've done it twice and I'm still alive. You know what that tells me, Uncle Wonderful? You're a coward. So, here's the deal. Either be a man and kill me, or get the hell out of my way."

He didn't say a word.

"Well?" I asked. "I'm waiting."

Uncle Wonderful stepped aside and said, "Get the hell out of here."

"Nothing would give me greater pleasure."

I went back inside and found Roy and Vinny smoking weed with a one hitter. They blew the smoke into a plastic garbage bag, and Vinny released it out a side window.

"Pretty ingenious, huh?" Vinny said, closing the bag. "If that sheriff comes back, he won't have a clue."

He's not the only one without a clue, I wanted to say. I turned to my cousin and there was a tear rolling down his cheek. "Okay," I said. "Now that your mom's gone tell me how it's really going?"

Roy let out a long, dope-scented sigh and said, "Like the world just ended, and I'm the one responsible. Thank God I'm high on Oxy, otherwise I'd be seriously depressed right now."

"That sounds more like it," I said. "What happened last night?"

"Jackie was giving me a foot job, and I lost control of the car."

"Really?" Vinny asked. "You didn't tell me that part."

"That's because it didn't happen, you idiot. Jesus, Vinny, you're the most gullible person I've ever met."

Roy was starting to lose it, and I put a hand on his shoulder. "So, how *is* your mom handling this?" I asked.

"You saw her. I mean, what would your mother say if the cops pulled you out of a car and there was a dead girl beside you?"

"I'll let you know next time it happens."

"Do that."

I was surprised by how easy it was to joke about Roy's crash, but that's what life had begun to feel like—one big joke. Jackie was dead, my mother was in a mental institution, and Roy was going to jail. And thanks to my fight with Uncle Wonderful, I had just said good-bye to my future. I tried to picture a happy alternative, but all I saw was despair.

Can things get any worse? I wondered.

Don't answer that, I immediately thought. *Things are bad enough already.*

17

IN THE MARKET FOR A FUN-FILLED AND EXCITING SPOT TO spend Christmas? Then I recommend avoiding mental hospitals at all costs. Unfortunately, that's exactly where I found myself on the morning of December 25, sipping fat-free eggnog and watching a conga line of drugged-out zombies doing a yuletide version of the Shady Oaks Shuffle. I could hardly wait until New Year's.

To be fair, Christmas was never a big deal around our house. This was for practical as well as religious reasons. With every library, department store, and government office closed for the holidays, there was nothing around worth stealing, and even my mother couldn't generate much enthusiasm for breaking into people's homes on Christmas. But there was more to it than that. If there was ever a day when the absence of a father in my life was most heartbreakingly apparent, it was on Christmas. Every

December I told myself that *this* was going to be the year my father slid down the chimney and transformed us into a real family. It never happened, and my mother and I usually spent Christmas morning watching TV, munching on candy canes, and counting the minutes until we could go to Uncle Wonderful's for dinner.

Shady Oaks had plenty of candy canes, but the trip to Uncle Wonderful's was out of the question because my mother was not allowed to leave. This was fine by me. I had other plans, and as mouthwatering as Aunt Marie's Christmas pork roast and linguine with clam sauce could be, I found the prospect of seeing Claire far more appetizing. Besides, after my fight with Uncle Wonderful, I figured my chances of returning to Wheaton were close to zero, and this would be my last opportunity to be alone with Claire. I tried not to dwell on it as I boarded the train at Grand Central, but with only drunken holiday revelers and spectacular views of the Hudson to distract me on the train ride north, it was all I could think about. We pulled into the Saratoga station twenty minutes late, and when I saw Claire waiting for me on the platform I practically catapulted off the train.

"Merry Christmas," she said, wrapping her arms around me.

"And a very *Feliz Navidad* to you."

Claire took a step back and said, "I can't believe you're actually here. C'mon, I have a surprise for you."

"Me first," I said, and handed Claire a small box.

"What is it?" she asked.

"Open it and find out."

Claire tore into the wrapping paper, and when she saw what was inside she actually shrieked.

"Holy Crap Balls! It's just like the one I lost!" She reached into the box and pulled out a tiny gold horseshoe for her charm bracelet. It cost most of what I'd earned in the cafeteria that fall, but just seeing the joy on Claire's face was worth it.

She held up the charm to take a closer look. "How did you know what it looked like?"

"I could tell you, but then I'd have to kill Santa."

"No, really. How did you figure it out?"

"I found an old picture of you on Facebook and blew it up. The charm was a little blurry, but I found a company on the Internet that could reproduce it and I guess they did an okay job."

"They did a *fantastic* job," she said, hugging me. "Thank you. Thank you so much."

"What's your surprise?" I asked.

Claire reached into her pocketbook and handed me a small gift bag covered in mistletoe. I stuck my hand inside and pulled out a brand-new iPhone.

"It's good to go," she said with a grin. "I set all the preferences, and it's linked to my father's corporate account so you don't have to worry about the bill."

"You sure that's okay?"

"There are so many phones on that account he won't even notice it. Push the button on the front and swipe up from the bottom."

I did as she told me, and a music player appeared on the screen. I pressed Play and a Foo Fighters track blasted from the iPhone's tiny speaker.

"Wow," I said.

"I filled it with all your favorite songs, and there's a fifty-dollar credit in your iTunes account for apps and more music."

"This is awesome," I said

"It's for my benefit as well as yours. Now we can text each other and do FaceTime whenever we want."

I followed Claire into the parking lot and looked around for her father's Mercedes. We stopped in front of a new BMW instead, and Claire pulled out her keys.

"Is this yours?" I asked.

Claire nodded.

"And you got it today?"

She nodded again.

My heart deflated. Next to a forty-five-thousand-dollar BMW, the charm I had bought her was nothing.

Claire must have read my mind and said, "It's just a car, Cam. I still like your present best."

"I guess . . ."

"No, I mean it. You went to a huge amount of trouble finding that charm. My father probably had his secretary order this over the phone."

"Thanks," I said, not really believing her.

"Want to drive it?"

I stared at the car before me. The prospect of driving a

spanking new Bavarian pleasure mobile was too good to pass up. "Sure," I said.

She tossed me the keys, and we hopped inside. Claire paired my iPhone to the BMW's sound system, and music poured from the car's sixteen hidden speakers. I'd thought my Mustang was fun to drive, but Claire's BMW was even better, and as we blew past the horse farms and palatial estates north of Albany, I forgot all about Princeton and my family and not going back to Wheaton. It was just the wheel in my hands, the road at my feet, and the beautiful woman beside me. And for a little while I was happy. Really, truly happy.

It took forty-five minutes to get to Claire's house, and when I saw where she lived I nearly passed out. At school, Claire's wealth was way more abstract. Sure, she had expensive clothes and a nice computer, but we both lived in the same dumpy dorms and ate in the same soggy cafeteria. Chateau Benson, on the other hand, told an entirely different story. I eased the BMW to a stop and stared at the twenty-room behemoth before me.

"You actually live here?" I asked.

"Just until they finish renovating the big house."

"Really?"

"No, not really. Of course I live here. Pull up ahead, we don't have much time until the party starts."

I was hoping this meant we were going to read Claire's essay (not to mention the Possibility of Expulsion), but for some silly reason she wanted to show me around. I parked the BMW in the four-car garage and followed her down a brick path to the stables.

That's right, I said stables.

"This is Crayola," she said, trotting out a massive brown stallion. "I've been riding him since I was ten and I love him like crazy. So try not to be jealous."

I gave Crayola the once-over and froze when I saw what he was packing between his horsey thighs. *Damn*, I thought. Is there anything about this place that's not intimidating?

"What do you think?" Claire asked.

"He's, uh, huge."

"He's not that big. Wait a minute. Don't tell me you've never been this close to a horse before?"

"Does a pony ride count?"

"My God, what do people on Long Island do all day?"

"Steal cars. Worship Satan. You know, the usual stuff. But seriously, I can't believe you actually climb on top of that thing. Do you get nosebleeds from the altitude?"

Claire pointed at me and smiled. "I think someone here needs a riding lesson."

"Not in a million years."

"You're not scared, are you?"

"Of course, I'm scared. A horse's brain is way too small for the size of its body. It's a scientific fact."

I was about to make a crack about the size of Crayola's crayon, then thought better of it. Some things are better left unsaid. Besides, Claire was already putting Crayola back in his parking spot—or whatever it is you call the place where horses sleep at night. Nursery? Solarium? Whatever.

Next up was a tour of the house. It's embarrassing to admit, but the first thing that popped into my head was what a fantastic time I would have had robbing it. After a few minutes, however, my attitude began to change. There was something about being in the very place where Claire grew up that was almost hypnotic, and I felt this incredible desire to have known her as a child. I wanted to travel back in time and be with her when she took her first step and gave her first doll a haircut. I wanted to be her high school boyfriend and witness every part of her life simultaneously. The feeling was overwhelming and I knew—right then and there—that I would have to take Roy's job.

It's the only way, I told myself. Yes, there was a strong chance my family would pull some kind of stunt, but that didn't matter. I wanted to live with Claire in a world of stables and horses, and if that meant going up against my family so be it.

Does it come as no surprise that I hated Claire's friends? Every Amber, Tiffany, and Scott Merriweather the Third ("Scottso to my friends, bro.") made me more jealous than the next, and it took less than ten minutes to break the vow of sobriety I'd made lying on the pee-pee protector on my mother's bathroom floor. I'd never had a gin and tonic before, but it went down fast and cool, and that's all that mattered.

The only problem was the more I drank, the more I felt

like a fraud. I tried to act like Cam Smith, but every time I opened my mouth Skip O'Rourke came pouring out. It made no sense. These were the same kind of people I'd been shining on for three-and-a-half years at Wheaton, but after just one week with my family I'd lost the ability to communicate with them. It was like I'd been infected by a virus. Except there was more to it than that. There was something about the way Claire and her friends carried themselves that I found more intoxicating than gin. They moved with this air of effortless certainty that seemed to say no matter what happened to them everything was going to turn out just super-duper, and that all the good jobs, fancy houses, and beautiful spouses were just waiting there for them to pluck off the tree of good fortune.

And damn it if I didn't want to be just like them.

Finally, thanks to a cocktail of one part resentment and two parts envy, I was driven from the party. I found a window seat on the second floor and stared down at the river of luxury vehicles clogging the driveway. *Look at that*, I told myself. The sticker price of just one of those cars would solve my problems three times over. I shook my head. Maybe it took one to know one, but something about their wealth struck me as almost criminal.

"Here you are."

I looked up, and Claire was standing it the doorway.

"Hey," I said.

She joined me at the window. "Having a good time?" she asked. "You seem a little preoccupied."

"I'm just tired."

"Maybe this party wasn't such a good idea."

"No, it's great."

She ran a hand through my hair and adjusted the curtains. "I love this spot. When I was a little girl I used to hide up here for hours. One time my parents even called the police."

The P word rattled my brain, and I stared into Claire's eyes. Her pupils filled me with awe, and I wanted to hide inside them forever. Then the craziest thought occurred to me, and for one drunken moment, I thought I'd discovered the answer to all my problems.

"Marry me," I blurted out.

"What?"

I grabbed Claire's hand and got down on my knees. "Claire Benson, will you marry me?"

"You mean now?"

"There must be a Justice of the Peace or a sea captain around here someplace. I'll defer my admission to Princeton and get some kind of job to support us. On weekends we can go for drives in the country, or go skiing, or do anything you want. It'll be magic. It'll be great."

"What kind of job will you get?" Claire asked.

"I don't know. I can work at a Home Depot or something."

She pulled me up from the floor. "How many drinks have you had?"

"Not too many. Why?"

"Are you crazy? You just got accepted to Princeton. Why would you want to work at Home Depot?"

"It'll only be until you graduate. After that, I'll get a job at a bank or something. Don't you want to get married?"

"Well, it's always been my dream to be proposed to by a man who's so drunk he might ask Crayola to marry him if I say no." She grabbed my chin. "What's the matter? You look like you're about to cry."

"I do not."

"Yes, you do. Is everything okay?"

My mind flashed to Fat Nicky and what would happen if the job went south. "I sure hope so . . ." I mumbled.

A look of concern crossed Claire's face. "Cam, is there something you're not telling me?"

"Of course not."

"Good, you had me scared for a second." But she didn't look convinced.

To change the subject, I put my head on her shoulder and said, "You have nothing to worry about. Everything's going to be fine."

I, on the other hand, had plenty to worry about including a sick mother, a vengeful uncle, and a cousin facing a manslaughter charge—to name my top three. Add to that an ex-mobster who wanted me to kill a man for him, and my life was a certifiable disaster. Lucky for me I was too exhausted to deal with any of it and passed out ten minutes later. So much for reading Claire's essay or the

Possibility of Expulsion. The good news was I didn't have to say good-bye to her friends. The bad news, as I learned the next morning, is that a gin hangover makes a beer hangover feel like a group hug from a busload of cheerleaders.

18

"THERE HE IS!" MR. DENUNSIO SAID WHEN I WALKED INTO his room on my first night as an employee of Shady Oaks. My hours were twelve at night to eight in the morning, and as far as temporary jobs went, it wasn't half bad. Yes, I had to mop floors and scrub toilets, but I was totally unsupervised and had plenty of free time to hang out with Mr. DeNunsio and plan a murder I had no intention of committing.

"You wanna drink, kid?" he asked as I closed the door behind me.

"No thanks, I'm not supposed to drink while on duty."

"On duty?" he said with a laugh. "What are you doing? Guarding the mop bucket?"

"Gimme a break. I just got this job."

"Then you better start off on the right foot." He pulled a bottle from his nightstand and held it up for inspection.

"Anisette, straight from the old country." He poured shots into two plastic tumblers and handed me one. I held it to my nose, and it smelled like a combination of licorice and paint thinner.

"Salute!" He threw back his drink with a single gulp and punched himself on the chest. "Damn, I wish my gut was in better shape so I could have a little Scotch once in a while."

I took a sip of the anisette, and it burned my throat like industrial-strength mouthwash. While I tried to regain the ability to speak, Mr. DeNunsio pulled an asthma inhaler from his robe and sucked the mist deep into his lungs.

"There," he said with a cough. "That's better." Then he grabbed a pack of Virginia Slims off his nightstand and lit one up.

"Just out of curiosity," I asked. "What's the point of using an asthma inhaler if you're going to smoke a cigarette afterward?"

Mr. DeNunsio shook his head and laughed. "What are you? Stupid? The inhaler is to open my lungs *for* the cigarette."

I laughed until I remembered what I was doing there, and the laugh died in my throat. This was the part of the job I hated most. The lying. Even at four years old I felt dirty making friends with people I knew I was going to rob. And yet, like most things I did as a kid, I was good at it.

"I almost forgot," Mr. DeNunsio said. "I have something for you." He reached into his robe and handed me an envelope. I tore it open and found five twenty-dollar bills inside.

"What's this for?" I asked.

"Road Runner."

"What?"

"That horse you told me to bet on last week. That's your cut."

I tried to hand back the money. "I don't deserve this."

"The hell you don't. I was all set to lay down a C-note on Sandy's Pride. Well, guess what? Sandy's Pride stopped to smell the roses, and Road Runner paid out five-to-one. Your advice made a six-hundred-dollar difference in my finances."

I put the money in my pocket. All I needed were sixty more Road Runners and I could return to school without pretending to kill someone.

"Thanks," I said.

"Listen, son. There are two types of money in this world—easy money and hard money. And the only difference between a millionaire and a bum is the millionaire knows easy money pays the bills just as well. *Capisce?*"

I nodded. "*Capisce.*"

"Good, now let's get to work."

"First I have a question."

Mr. DeNunsio raised an eyebrow. "Only one?"

"One to begin with."

"Okay, shoot."

"Why us? I mean, why my family and not some professional?"

He took a last drag off of his cigarette and dropped it in a coffee mug. "Two reasons. The first is your family isn't part of the mob. You hear all this stuff about honor and vows of silence, but it's a myth. Everybody talks. It wouldn't matter if I was in freaking Afghanistan, two minutes after I asked a goombah to whack Fat Nicky, ten guys would be talking about it on Mulberry Street. Second, and the main reason, is I can't afford anyone else. Sure, I've got a few bucks in the bank, but this place is expensive, and I plan on living a lot longer. A real hit would wipe me out. Any more questions?"

"Not for now."

"Good." He reached into his nightstand and pulled out a photograph. "Okay, this is where he lives."

I stared at the photo, and something about the house looked familiar. "Where is this place?" I asked.

"About three miles from here."

"On Pine Wood Drive?"

"You know it?"

Of course I knew it. Fat Nicky lived less than five blocks from the Cheshire Arms, the apartment complex I had almost burned down as a kid.

"Yeah, my mom and I used to live nearby."

"Damn. That complicates things. You're a known quantity there."

I shook my head. "It was a long time ago. Besides, I know the area like the back of my hand. The yards, the canals, everything."

"Canals?"

"Yeah, the backyards go straight to the water and are connected by canals instead of alleyways."

"No kidding?" he said. "That might work in our favor. You can swim, right?"

"Like a fish."

"Good deal." He pulled out a second photograph and handed it to me. "That's him."

I took the picture and sized up the man I was supposed to kill. Fat Nicky was around seventy-five years old and his face was dotted with age spots. He looked tired and frail, and the first word that popped into my head was "grandpa." I tried to hand back the picture, but Mr. DeNunsio refused take it.

"Look a little longer," he said. "Memorize it. Because after tonight, neither of us can have a picture of him in our possession."

I stared at the photo and asked, "How come they call him Fat Nicky? He doesn't look that fat to me."

"He lost a lot of weight after he got shot."

"Then why do they still call him *fat*?"

"Once you get a nickname you're stuck with it."

"What's yours?"

"Sally Broccoli."

"Sally Broccoli?" I said with a laugh. "How did you end up with a name like that?"

"I used to work with my pop selling vegetables at the Hunts Point Market. Some wiseass came up with the name and it stuck."

"I guess it's better than Tony Toe Cheese."

"You can say that again." He took the picture and tore it into little pieces. "And just to give you a taste of the kind of person we're dealing with here, the first thing Fat Nicky made me do after I joined his crew was shake down my pop for protection money."

"Did you do it?"

"You don't say no to these guys."

"What happened?"

"He made me break three of my father's fingers. One at a time."

"Jesus."

Mr. DeNunsio sighed and reached for the anisette bottle. "Trust me, son. Jesus had nothing to do with it."

19

AS MUCH FUN AS IT WAS HANGING OUT WITH MR. DENUNSIO and planning a make-believe murder, I was totally exhausted by the end of my shift. I wanted to visit my mother, but there was zero gas left in my tank, and I was worried I'd fall asleep on the bus ride home. I was so tired, in fact, I didn't notice the scruffy guy with tattoos hanging out near the employees' entrance.

"Hey," he said.

"What the hell?" I said, jumping back. "Don't scare a person like that."

"Sorry. You Roy?"

"No."

"They said the new guy's name was Roy."

"It was. But Roy got in a car wreck, and I'm the *new* new guy. Who are you?"

"I'm the old old guy." He stuck out a hand. "Frank Quinn."

I shook his hand and said, "Skip O'Rourke. How come you quit?"

"I didn't quit. I got fired."

"Why?"

"You tell me. They said it was for stealing drugs, but that's bullshit. I mean, I *was* stealing drugs, but I'd been doing that for years. Somebody must have said something."

"Who?" I asked.

"That's what I wanted to talk to Roy about, but since he's not here I'll ask you." He got in my face and said, "So, tell me, Skip O'Rourke. Why did I get fired?"

I looked him in the eyes and said, "The hell if I know. My mother's a patient in the O'Neil Pavilion, and I'm just filling in until they find somebody permanent."

My answer seemed to satisfy him, and he took a step back. "It's not a bad job, actually."

"If you like the smell of pee."

"Well, there's that," he said with a laugh. "To be honest, I got to the point where I couldn't smell it anymore."

"Hopefully, it won't get to that point for me." I nodded at the Lincoln Navigator parked behind him and said, "Nice car."

"Thanks. I'm about to lose it."

"Why?"

"The money I made off the meds I stole went to the payments. Now I work in a furniture store, and the stuff's too big to steal."

"Life can be challenging that way."

"That's the other reason I'm here. I have clients who still need pills. Want to go into business with me?"

I gave him the once-over. Even if I was stupid enough to sell drugs there was no way I'd do it with somebody like Frank. Then my mind flashed to the pills in my mother's medicine cabinet, and I thought about selling him those. Except that was a dumb idea, too, and smelled way too much like something an O'Rourke would do. I shook my head. "Thanks, but I don't think so."

"It's easy money. The inventory system here sucks, and the only reason I got caught was that somebody didn't know how to keep their mouth shut."

I hopped off the loading dock. "Sorry, Frank, I don't deal drugs."

"Okay, but could you do me a favor? If you happen to find out who ratted on me would you give me a call?"

"Sure," I said, and entered his number in my iPhone. It was all an act because I already knew who had ratted him out: my mother. While not surprising, this struck me as more than a little hypocritical considering the lesson she'd given me on the same subject thirteen years earlier.

We were working the Fine Jewelry counter at the Macy's, and as my mother asked the saleslady to show her an expensive gold bracelet, I turned around and jammed an entire pack of Little Debbie Cloud Cakes into my mouth. This was no small feat considering I was only four years old, but I'd spent two days practicing and had mastered the fine art of stuffing my face without gagging. I chewed and chewed, and on my mother's cue I began spitting up Cloud Cake all over the place.

"Oh my God," the saleslady shrieked. "Is he all right?"

Of course I was all right, and so was my mother who took advantage of the saleslady's concern to swap the gold bracelet in her hand with a fake one from Target.

"I'm so sorry," my mother said when the switch was complete. "Is there a bathroom around here someplace?"

"On the second floor."

"Can you make it that far, honey?" she asked.

"No," I replied in the most pathetic voice I could muster. "I think I'm gonna be sick again."

"Then I better take you outside." She lifted me up, and as we headed for the exit she turned back to the saleslady and said, "Can you put that bracelet on hold for me until tomorrow? My name is Fisher. Martha Fisher."

"Hurry, Mama," I moaned. "Hurry, please."

The key to this scam was getting the saleslady to put the bracelet in the hold bin as quickly as possible. Even a mediocre salesperson can spot a fake piece of jewelry after a couple of minutes, and at a high-end place like Macy's it takes less than that. Unfortunately, my mother failed to notice the white carnation pinned to the saleslady's blouse. A white carnation is Macy's code for a senior manager, which meant the woman had been dealing with weasels for years. We were barely halfway across the store when an alert went out over the PA system, and security came after us.

"Listen, Sonny," my mother whispered as she slipped

the real bracelet into my jeans. "The guards are going to grab me, but I want you to keep on running. Don't stop until you get away, then find a pay phone and call Grandpa Patsy. He'll know what to do."

"I'm scared, Mama."

"I know you are, baby. Just do what I said and everything will be okay. Quick, what's Grandpa Patsy's phone number?"

"555-7396."

"Good." She squeezed my arm and said, "Here come the security guards. Are you going to be a big boy for Mama?"

"I'll try."

"Trying's not good enough. Here they are. Now RUN!"

She set me down, and I raced for the door. As I pulled it open, I looked back and saw two beefy security guards knock my mother to the ground and twist her arms behind her back. I was terrified, but I did exactly as I was told. I ran, and ran, and kept on running until I found a Burger King and scrambled inside. I pulled out the emergency quarter hidden in my shoe, climbed on a pile of booster seats, and dialed the only telephone number I knew by heart.

But somehow I blew it. I'm not sure if I got the number wrong, or if my little fingers were shaking so badly I pressed the wrong button by accident. All I know is that the person who answered the phone wasn't Grandpa Patsy, and I hung up.

Now what am I supposed to do? I wondered. I had no other money, my mother was in custody, and there was a stolen bracelet in my pants. I thought about sneaking up on some old lady and stealing her pocketbook, but even old ladies were bigger than me. *Think*, I told myself. There has to be something you can do. Then I remembered the fountain back at the mall. Not only was it filled with hundreds of dimes and quarters, but it was right across from the Mrs. Field's cookie stand. I could scoop up some change, call Grandpa Patsy, and still have money left over for a cookie. It was the first plan I had ever thought of, and I felt like a criminal mastermind.

Or I did until my plan backfired. I don't know what happened, but one moment I was reaching for a big juicy quarter, and the next I was falling headfirst into the fountain. The water tasted like oven cleaner, and my eyes burned like someone had doused them with chili powder. It was easily the worst thing that had ever happened to me, and by the time I crawled out of the fountain two mall cops were waiting for me.

"Where's your mother, little boy?" the first one asked.

I knew I wasn't supposed to tell them, but I didn't know what else to do. I was four years old, drenched, alone, and scared.

"Macy's," I whimpered.

The police were there when I arrived and when they pulled the gold bracelet from my jeans I thought they were going to kiss me. Talk about perfect timing, they were about to release my mother for lack of evidence, but thanks to me, they now had everything they needed to arrest us for shoplifting. Or at least arrest my mother, because you can't arrest a four-year-old—although that didn't stop them from slapping handcuffs on my wrists and marching me out the door where a photographer for *Newsday* was waiting to capture my shame for the next day's paper. Our next stop was the Seventh Precinct where my mother was charged with Petit Larceny, and I got to play Go Fish with a lady detective because the cops didn't know what else to do with me.

Aunt Marie had to bail us out because Uncle Wonderful was in prison for mail fraud and Grandpa Patsy was highly allergic to police stations. But Grandpa Patsy was there when we got home, and he was nice enough to hold me down while my mother spanked me until her hand went numb.

"You stupid shit!" she shrieked. "You stupid little shit!"

"This is for your own good, Skipper," Grandpa Patsy whispered in my ear. "Nobody likes a rat, and the sooner you learn that the better. Now say it."

"Nobody likes a rat!" I cried.

"Again."

"Nobody. Likes. A. Rat."

"Good. Now never forget it."

20

MR. DENUNSIO'S IDEA TO ACCESS FAT NICKY'S HOUSE VIA the canals was a good one. Nobody would be expecting that. A boat? Maybe. But a lone swimmer on an icy December night? Not in a million years. Still, the plan was not without its challenges. First off, I'd have to find a wet suit in December. Not totally impossible, but the selection would be limited, and I'd have to pay for it with cash. I'd also need a car and a gun, but my biggest problem was finding a partner. Vinny was the obvious choice, the main reason being I didn't know anyone else. The Vinster wasn't the smartest criminal on the South Shore, but with his shaved head, tattoos, and nervous eyes he certainly looked the part. Roy didn't want him involved with the job for some reason, but I didn't care. I needed a warm body, and Vinny was available.

I called him to hang out, and he arrived five minutes

early. Always a good sign. Our first stop was a liquor store where Vinny bought a pint of Jack Daniel's, and I got a half pint of Jägermeister because I'd heard guys at school talking about it. I didn't plan on drinking any, but I figured it would make me look more like an adult when I asked Vinny to do the job. Neither of us felt like going to a bar, and there weren't any good movies playing, so we drove around until we wound up at an indoor mini golf in Deer Park. Vinny inhaled most of his Jack Daniel's on the way, and by the time we finished the third hole his bottle was empty.

"You want a hit of this?" I asked, holding out my Jägermeister. "It's not bad in a cough-syrupy kind of way."

Vinny shook his head.

I slipped the bottle in my pocket and, as I lined up my shot, it occurred to me that Vinny hadn't said a word since we had arrived.

"What's the matter, buddy?" I asked.

"I don't know," Vinny said, hugging himself. "It just feels wrong not having Roy with us."

"I was just thinking the same thing myself."

"It's just so messed up. One minute Roy's driving around like any other night, and the next minute Jackie's dead. It doesn't make any sense. I mean, why him? Why not you, or me, or the man in the moon?"

"You got me. I guess that's why people go to church. It's the only thing there is to explain all the crazy stuff in the world."

Vinny nodded, but I could tell he wasn't buying my two sentence summary of the Religion and Popular Culture class I'd taken that fall. Not that I blamed him. One of the worst things about being a criminal is you never get to feel that God is on your side. That said, every weasel I knew relied on some kind of routine or good luck charm to help keep them out of jail. Grandpa Patsy was the worst. Not only did he go to church every week to dip his lucky Irish shilling in holy water, but he never wore purple on a job, and refused to talk business during Lent—although that never stopped him from calling his bookie ten times a day to check the point spread.

Like so many things with my family, this drove me totally insane. I mean, what was the point of going to church on Sunday if you planned on robbing the poor box on Monday? My mother, naturally, had an explanation for this.

"You have to understand something, Sonny," she said one afternoon as we walked out of a dry cleaner with another customer's clothing. "God sees what we're doing, and even though He's not a hundred percent happy with it, He forgives us as long as we don't steal from the wrong kind of people. Take these clothes for example. Do you think God would let us take them if He didn't want us to? I mean really, what kind of woman buys a four-hundred-dollar ball gown that needs to be dry cleaned every time she wears it?"

"A woman with a lot of money?"

"Exactly. And like it says in the Bible, rich people and camels never get into heaven."

"I'm glad to see all those years in Catholic school paid off," I said, shaking my head.

"Hey!" someone behind Vinny and me shouted. "Are you guys gonna play golf, or what?"

We turned around, and a guy in a Celtics jacket was standing on the next green with his girlfriend.

"Give us a break," Vinny shouted back. "We're having a serious discussion here!"

"Then let us play through."

Vinny looked down at his ball and kicked it to the end of the green. "There. Does that make you happy?"

"What a dickhead," the girlfriend said.

"What was that?" Vinny growled.

"You heard what I said."

Vinny pointed his golf club at the guy and said, "I'd put that dog on a shorter leash if I were you, pal."

I grabbed Vinny's arm. "Yo, chill."

"Screw you," the guy said.

Vinny laughed. "Screw me? Screw you! Step over here, and I'll pound every tooth out of your mouth."

The guy barreled toward us and when he got within striking distance Vinny swung his club at him. He missed by a mile, and before he could take another swing the guy punched him in the stomach. Vinny's legs went out from under him and he fell to the ground coughing.

"Asshole," the girlfriend said as they marched past us to the next green.

I squatted down next to Vinny. "You okay, man?"

"I could use a hit of that Jägermeister, if you don't mind."

I handed him the bottle, and he guzzled down the entire thing.

"You sure that's a good idea?" I asked.

"Are you kidding? It's the best idea I've had all day," he said as he jumped up, ran to the next green, and slipped his golf club across the guy's throat.

"There," Vinny shouted, squeezing the club as hard as he could. "How does that feel? Huh? Huh?"

The girlfriend screamed and dug her fingernails into Vinny's forearm. "Stop it! You're killing him!"

I ran to the green and pulled the club out of Vinny's hands. The guy fell to the ground, and Vinny put his heel on the guy's neck.

"One word," Vinny hissed. "One word and I'll make you a quadriplegic."

The guy remained silent, and Vinny lifted his foot.

"Pussy," he said with a grin.

Someone turned off the music, and I looked up to see everyone at the golf course staring at us. People were reaching for their cell phones, and I figured it was only a matter of seconds before they began posting our pictures online.

"C'mon, Vin," I said. "Let's get out of here."

"Sure thing, Skip."

I had Vinny drop me off at home, which was kind of stupid considering how drunk he was, but I didn't care. I just wanted to get away from the guy. The moment he drove away, however, I remembered the buses to Shady Oaks had stopped running for the night. Yes, I could have called a cab, but Vinny's rampage had unnerved me and all I wanted to do was crawl under my *Star Wars* sheets and call Claire.

Which was exactly what I did. We talked deep into the night, and when we were done I took a couple of silly selfies and texted them to her. As I dozed off it occurred to me why Roy didn't want Vinny involved in the Mr. DeNunsio job, and I couldn't have agreed with him more because the last thing you need on any job—real or pretend—is a psychopath for a wingman.

"Where the hell were you last night?" Mr. DeNunsio hissed when I walked in his room the following evening.

"It's a little hard to explain," I said, stopping in my tracks.

"No, it's not. You were supposed to be here and you weren't. See? Easy peasy."

I stared at Mr. DeNunsio, and my mind flashed to my compromised morals, family psycho drama, and Vinny almost strangling that guy with his golf club. I didn't want or ask for any of it, but I was doing my best to hold it all together, and now I was getting grief for it. It was time to take a stand.

"You know what else is easy peasy?" I said under my breath. "Telling you to kiss my butt. If you don't like what I'm doing go find somebody else to kill Fat Nicky for you." I turned and headed for the door.

"Wait a minute!" he said. "Get back here."

"Why?" I asked. "Why should I listen to a single word you say?"

Mr. DeNunsio reeled in his anger and said, "I'm sorry I yelled at you. Grab a seat and we can talk this thing through."

I folded my arms across my chest. "I'd rather stand."

"Suit yourself, but let me ask you a question. What if somebody from Shady Oaks saw you last night? Yeah, I know it's a long shot, but stranger things have happened. Wouldn't they have wondered, even a little bit, why you were out messing around when you should have been at work?"

"Maybe," I said with a shrug.

"You're damned straight they'd wonder, and that's all it takes. It might seem like nothing right now, but let me tell you how it works. You add up ten little nothings and pretty soon you got one big something that lands your ass in jail. And if that happens, there are two other things you gotta remember. The first is that if you get caught, prison is the least of your worries. Twenty years in a jumpsuit is nothing compared to what the pasta eaters would do if they found out you killed one of their own. They wouldn't think twice about killing your mother and feeding your uncle his cojones for breakfast. And the other thing is, if they get you, they get me. And I don't wanna get got. You hear me?"

I nodded.

"Good." He reached into his nightstand and pulled out the anisette. "You wanna drink?"

"I think I'll pass."

"Still playing the hard ass, huh?"

"No," I said. "I honestly don't like it."

"Fair enough." He poured himself a drink and said, "And just so you know the kind of people we're dealing with here, let me tell you a little story. You know who Rudy Giuliani is, right?"

"The mayor from 9/11?"

"That's him, but before that he ran the US Attorney's office in New York. He and his storm troopers had a major hard-on for the mob, and they invested a ton of time looking for people to help them bust it open. They needed guys who were high up in the ranks, but who didn't have any real power of their own. Guys like me. One day they hauled me in and laid it out. They had all the evidence needed to nail me with an extortion rap, and I was looking at four, maybe five years in prison. Then they made me an offer: If I testified against Fat Nicky, they'd drop the charges and give me and my family a new identity. If I didn't, it was jail. I knew I shouldn't have listened to their crap, but after a while I started to believe them. If they had their act together, I might have gotten away clean, but Nicky got off on a loophole and never even spent a night in jail."

Mr. DeNunsio sniffed back a tear then pulled out his inhaler and lit a cigarette. "Three years and two months later I was at work when the phone rang. It was the police calling to say there'd been an accident, and my entire family had been blown to pieces. They said it was a gas leak, but I knew different. It was Fat Nicky's way of making me suffer for the rest of my life."

"That's insane," I whispered.

"Insane or not, that's what these guys do when you cross them." He emptied his glass and said, "So, consider yourself warned. And the next time you feel like doing something stupid just remember you could get us all killed. *Capisce?*"

I looked straight at him and did my best not to blink. "*Capisce.*"

21

DR. BRAUNSTEIN INTERCEPTED ME A FEW HOURS LATER ON my way home from work. I'd been avoiding my mother's doctor for days because I didn't want to hear how it was all my fault that she had tried to kill herself. I also didn't know what kind of lies she had been telling him in her therapy sessions, and I didn't want to get our stories crossed. That said, my real reason for avoiding Dr. Braunstein was less complex: I was afraid of psychiatrists. To me, they were like brain police who could look into your head and see your darkest secrets. And for a guy whose life was built on a foundation of lies, that kind of scrutiny was terrifying.

Growing up, the worst thing about moving around so much was visiting the school psychiatrist every time I enrolled in a new district. At first, I made up all kinds of crazy stories like how I was part Navajo and that my father was killed in Iraq. But this strategy backfired big time, and I was rewarded for my creativity with even more trips to the school psychiatrist. After that, I learned that the best way to work the system was to tell the psychiatrists exactly what they wanted to hear.

Except here's the deal. Deep down, I *wanted* to tell them the truth. Because even in grade school I felt ashamed of who I was. I mean, what kind of family rents a hotel room for a week, visits every library within a twenty-mile radius, and applies for fake library cards so they can steal every DVD in town? Want to know what kind of family does that? Mine, of course. And the older I got the more frustrated I became by the sheer stupidity of my day-to-day existence. Take that little DVD caper, for example. How much money do you think we got for those DVDs? Three, maybe four bucks a pop depending on their condition. Subtract from that the money for the hotel, gas, and fake IDs, and we probably cleared less than ten bucks on the whole operation. Think about it. An entire town loses their DVD collection, and we made less than the cost of a single DVD. It was lunacy, absolute lunacy, and the fact that I couldn't tell anyone about it made me feel powerless and alone.

"You have a minute, Skip?"

I looked up and Dr. Braunstein was climbing out of a beat-up Outback in the parking lot.

"I was hoping to catch the S21 bus before rush hour gets crazy," I said, immediately regretting my use of the word "crazy" within a hundred yards of a psychiatrist.

“This will only take a minute,” he said. “Walk with me.”

Seeing no alternative, I did as I was told.

“What do you think?” he asked as we walked to the O’Neil Pavilion. “The Knicks going to take it this year?”

“Maybe,” I replied, surprised that Dr. Braunstein chose the Sports Opening to kick off our conversation. The Sports Opening—or the SO as I liked to call it—was a technique used by school psychologists to see if you were gay. I had no idea what me being gay or not had to do with my mother’s mental condition, but that didn’t prevent me from giving the good doctor my standard reply.

“It’s a little early in the season to tell,” I said, pretending to think about it for a moment. “But they’ve got a pretty good bench, and as long as their shooters stay healthy I’d say they’ve got a decent chance.”

Dr. Braunstein nodded, and I watched him check off the little Straight box in his head. I was pleased with my response, but also a bit disappointed that he’d opted for such a pedestrian opening. After all, his fee had cost me a Mustang.

“So, how do you think my mother is doing?” I asked.

“How do *you* think she’s doing?” he replied in perfect shrinkly fashion.

“I’m not sure,” I said. “I’ve been away for so long it’s hard to separate the mother in my memory from the person I see today.”

“Then let me be the first to tell you. She’s making real progress.”

"That's terrific news," I said. "When do you think she can be released?"

"It's still too early to say."

"I'll put it another way. Spring break starts the first week of March. Do you think she'll be okay by then?"

Dr. Braunstein scratched his beard and said, "If things continue the way they're going, March is not out of the question."

"And she won't try to kill herself again if I go back to school?"

He stared at me. "Your mother didn't try to kill herself because you went away to school."

"But that's what my uncle said."

"That's ridiculous. And even if it was true—which it's not—it would be completely irresponsible for him to say that."

"So why did she try to kill herself?"

"It's not really my place to discuss these things with you, Skip. Although I will say, she has a lot of unresolved guilt about her father, and her marriage, and the loss of her first child."

"I understand," I said, and this time I really did. Not that my mother harbored guilt over a dead child or failed marriage because those things never happened. What I understood was that she was spinning fairy tales for her doctor.

Dr. Braunstein opened the back door of the O'Neil Pavilion, and as we walked inside I almost felt sorry for the guy. He might have been a rube, but he was still trying to get to the bottom of my mother's problems. Unfortunately, none of them were real. Way to go, Mom.

We stopped at the reception area, and Dr. Braunstein pulled some letters from the mailboxes behind the desk. He thumbed through the envelopes and said, "I hope you're also making time to visit your father while you're home. It must be strange having both your parents here."

"Excuse me?"

"Your mother and your father. It must be strange having both of them here at Shady Oaks."

"My father's here?" I sputtered. "Where?"

"At the Williams Pavilion." Dr. Braunstein looked up from his mail. "You mean, you didn't know?"

"Of course I knew," I replied as nonchalantly as my pounding heart would allow. "I'm just so tired from working all night my brain isn't functioning properly."

Dr. Braunstein nodded. "I had the same problem when I used to work twenty-four-hour shifts as a resident. It was a miracle I was able to drive home sometimes."

"Have you spoken to my father much?" I asked, trying to pump Dr. Braunstein for more information.

"Just in passing. The Williams Pavilion has its own therapists on staff."

"He's quite the character, huh?"

"You can say that again."

Dr. Braunstein's phone rang and he checked the number. "Sorry, Skip, but I have to take this."

"Sure thing, Dr. Braunstein. It was nice talking to you."

"Right back at you, Skip. Don't be a stranger."

I left Dr. Braunstein to take his call and headed down the hallway to my mother's wing.

I visualized every male patient at the Williams Pavilion, and the obvious choice was Mr. DeNunsio. True, I could almost hear my Intro to Statistics instructor screaming "Correlation does not imply causation," but it didn't matter. My mother said she and Mr. DeNunsio were old friends, he occasionally called me son, and we kind of looked alike if you ignored my hair, nose, and lack of a mustache. But most of all, I *wanted* him to be my father.

I burst into my mother's room and found her in the bathroom brushing her teeth.

"Is Mr. DeNunsio my father?" I asked.

"Where'd you get that idea?"

"From Dr. Braunstein."

She spit out her toothpaste. "He wasn't supposed to tell you that."

"Is he?"

I could see the wheels spinning behind her eyes. "No."

"Then why does Dr. Braunstein think so? And what's all this nonsense about having a baby who died?"

"Let's sit down."

"I don't need to sit down."

"Well, I do," she said, shuffling out of the bathroom and sitting on the edge of her bed. She took a cigarette off her nightstand, remembered she didn't have any matches, and put it back in the pack.

"I'm waiting," I said.

"All right," she said with a sigh. "Three afternoons a week we have these group therapy sessions where we're supposed to talk about our problems and discuss them with the other patients."

"I know what group therapy is."

"So the other people in the group have these really boring stories about how their sisters took their favorite doll when they were girls, or how their husbands are more into golf than taking them to the symphony. Completely boring stuff. And all the while I'm saying to myself, 'This woman is an anorexic because of this?' Or, 'This guy had a nervous breakdown because of that?' And the worst part is they think these things are like earth-shattering events." She laughed. "If they knew half the stuff I've done they'd die of heart attacks right in their folding chairs. Except I can't tell them the truth, so I started making things up. First about this baby who died, then about Sal DeNunsio being your father."

Disappointment washed over me, and I felt like crying. Of course the story about Mr. DeNunsio was a lie. It came out of my mother's mouth. But instead of feeling angry at my mother, I felt sorry for her because I had done the same thing at Wheaton a thousand times over. Granted, my mother lied for weasely reasons, and I was just trying to live a normal life, but lying eats away at your soul no matter why you do it.

"C'mon, Mom," I said, "how do you expect to get better if you keep telling people stories?"

"I know, I know. It was fun at first, but now it's all anybody wants to talk about. I can't tell you how hard it is keeping all this stuff straight in my head. It's worse than being questioned by the police."

"At least you have some experience in that department."

"That doesn't make it any easier. Sometimes I feel like Sasquatch having to tell a new story every night."

"You mean Scheherazade."

"Whatever. It's still exhausting."

"You could try telling the truth."

She looked at me like I was the crazy one. "And what fun would that be?"

"Just a suggestion. And speaking of Dr. Braunstein, he said that it would be okay for me to go back to school next week."

"Oh really? And when did Dr. Braunstein become your mother?"

"About two seconds before Mr. DeNunsio became my father."

"Touché."

I joined my mother on the edge of the bed and took her hand. "Look, Ma, going back to school is really important to me, but this isn't going to be like last time. Spring Break is just a couple of months away, and I promise I'll come back and visit."

"All right."

"And now there's something else I want to talk to you about."

"What's that?"

"If you ever, I repeat, *ever* think about killing yourself again I want you to call me. I don't care where I am, or what time it is. Okay?"

"Okay."

"Say, 'I promise.' "

"I promise."

"Good," I replied, not knowing which was worse: If my family was scamming me, or if my mother had actually tried to kill herself.

22

THREE NIGHTS LATER I FOUND MYSELF HIDING IN A RED Lobster parking lot a mile from my house. It was two in the morning, and there was only one car remaining, which I assumed belonged to the night manager. I'd been crouching in the damp gravel since midnight, and my legs were cramped and throbbing.

"C'mon," I whispered. "Shut off the lights and go home already."

The back door opened, and a man in a rumpled suit walked out carrying a black garbage bag. He tossed the bag in a dumpster, slammed the lid, and climbed into his car. I watched as he drove away and counted to a hundred to make sure he was gone for good. It was super quiet outside, and as I tiptoed across the parking lot the gravel crunching beneath my feet sounded like thunder. I lifted the lid of the dumpster, and the first thing that struck me was the smell of rotting fish. It was overwhelming, and I had to put my hand over my mouth to keep from gagging. Next came the flies. Millions of them. In my eyes. In my hair. All over my skin. It was a good thing my mouth was closed, or I would have inhaled a dozen of them. My stomach lurched, and I had to jump back and rub my hands all over my body to get the sickening feeling of them off of me. I was surprised I didn't vomit.

It took me a few minutes to recover, but I gathered up my courage and approached the dumpster again. I sucked in a deep breath, put a hand over my mouth, and raised the lid. This time I was ready for the flies and turned my head away as they swarmed all over me. When most of them were gone, I switched on my Maglite and peered inside. The dumpster was filled with trash bags, cooking oil containers, and enough fish guts for five restaurants. I lifted a bag, and a fresh wave of flies washed over me. The tingling on my face and lips was the most disgusting sensation I'd ever experienced, and it seemed like forever before the flies finally buzzed off. It took two more fly-infested bag liftings before I gave up and accepted the sad fact that I'd have to climb inside the dumpster. With the exception of having my spleen removed with a lacrosse stick, this was the last thing on earth I wanted to do.

What's the big deal? my inner O'Rourke asked. It's only flies and garbage. It won't kill you.

Except some things are worse than death. Or at least that's what I thought as I climbed into the dumpster and my sneakers filled with goo. Words can't describe what it was like in there. Imagine your worst nightmare, supersize it, then add a double helping of gross. It was that bad. My lungs were bursting, and I was about to climb out to catch my breath when the beam of my Maglite crossed something that looked familiar. I kicked away some crab legs, pushed aside an oil tin, and there he was: Elmo! I put the Maglite in my mouth, reached into the muck, and pulled out a brown paper package covered with Sesame Street stickers. Success! I stuck the package under my arm and climbed out of the dumpster with my lungs about to explode.

Damn, I thought as I scraped a dozen shrimp shells off my legs. I'd rather pretend to kill ten ex-mobsters than have to do that again.

I slipped the package under my coat and headed home. The streets were quiet, and as I squished past the houses and yards, I wondered if any of my neighbors were awake and peering out of their windows. Where would they think I was coming from? From 7-Eleven? From seeing some girl? Certainly not from fishing a gun out of a garbage dumpster. Not me. Not the honors student, nationally ranked lacrosse player, and future graduate of Princeton University.

You wanna bet?

I glanced at the houses around me and tried to imagine what was happening behind their windows which were now so dark. After all, if Skip O'Rourke was a thief and make-believe killer, what did that make Betty Brown or

Johnny Jones? Drug dealers? Eco-terrorists? The possibilities were endless, and if there was one thing I'd learned during my Christmas vacation, it's that it doesn't matter how moral you think you are, once someone takes away what you love most in this world, you'll do almost anything to get it back.

Wasn't I the perfect example?

When I got home I took the longest and hottest shower I could stand then doused my clothes with kerosene and set them on fire. Okay, so maybe I didn't burn my clothes, but I totally would have if I had access to a blast furnace. Instead, I stuffed them in the washing machine and dumped in enough laundry detergent to sanitize the entire South Shore of Long Island. And when that was done, I planned on doing it again. In the meantime, I tore open the package and inspected my new gun.

It was a Walther PPK, and according to Wikipedia it was the same model pistol Adolf Hitler used to kill himself. This was an excellent recommendation for any firearm, but way more important for my purposes, it was the same make and model as the gun in Uncle Wonderful's closet and thus the only type of gun I was familiar with.

I picked up the Walther, and the first thing I noticed was a patch of freshly scraped metal where the serial numbers were supposed to be. *Okay*, I told myself. I have now officially broken the law. Everything up until now has been talk and easy to deny, but this was real. In my possession was a gun that was more than likely stolen and which the serial numbers were filed off. I was guilty of two crimes and I hadn't even left my bedroom.

A Walther weighs about two pounds, but this one felt lighter than expected. I pressed a button near the grip, and the ammo clip popped out and fell to the floor. I double-checked that it was empty and pulled back the action to inspect the chamber. Also empty.

It was time to play.

I clicked off the safety and held the gun in front of me. There was a metal bead at the front of the barrel and a metal *V* in the back. I lined up these two points and was pleased to see how little my hand shook. This was important. I looked around for something to shoot, and my eyes came to rest on a ribbon I'd won at the Neil Armstrong Elementary School science fair. My project had been a volcano made out of papier-mâché, and I would have won first place if my mother had remembered to buy baking soda for the lava. As luck would have it, she bought baking *powder*, and first place went to a girl named Kimberly Kim who had made a caveman diorama out of Barbie dolls and pictures from *National Geographic*. I still haven't forgiven either of them.

I lined up the sights on the ribbon, squeezed the trigger, and—*Click!*

Is that it? I wondered, dropping my hand to my side. Is that the difference between life and death? Just a little click that takes about as much effort as tying your shoe? I sat on the edge of my bed and thought about all the people that click had taken from the world—Abraham Lincoln, Mahatma Gandhi, John Lennon. Add to that the millions more who'd died for no other reason than being in the wrong place at the wrong time. The numbers were overwhelming. So much suffering, so much death, and all so pointless. I stared at the gun and was struck by the absurdity of my situation. While my fellow Wheatonians were off enjoying the slopes of Aspen and the beaches of St. Croix, I was digging through piles of fish guts and target practicing with an illegal firearm. It felt stupid even thinking the words, but it just didn't seem fair.

There's still time to get out, I told myself. You've done nothing irreversible. Possession is nine-tenths of the law, and if you lose possession of the gun, you lose possession of the crime. You can go back to being an honors student and lacrosse star again. It's not too late.

But it was, and I would have been foolish to think otherwise. As long as my family believed I had stolen Grandpa Patsy's money, they would not leave me alone until they got revenge. Any way I looked at it, the Mr. DeNunsio job was my only way out.

Of course, the real question was would my family leave me alone *after* the Mr. DeNunsio job? That was anyone's guess, and I held the gun tighter and tried not to think about it.

23

I TOOK A BUS TO SEE ROY THE FOLLOWING AFTERNOON. Between doctors, lawyers, and physical therapy sessions, he was super busy, but we eventually agreed on a time when I could drop by his parents' house and see how he was doing. Thanks to Claire's most generous Christmas present not only did I now have a phone number that my uncle couldn't hack, I also had access to the Internet. I Googled Fat Nicky Gangliosi and saw that Roy was correct about him having "a little lead in his chest." According to the *Daily News*, Fat Nicky had been shot five times in a failed assassination attempt at a steak house in Bay Ridge, Brooklyn. His bodyguards were killed within seconds, and the only thing that saved his life was his pushing over a table and using it for a shield.

When I got to Uncle Wonderful's house Roy was in his childhood bedroom watching a soccer game on a Spanish channel and chain-smoking Marlboros. He was pale, deflated, and looked like he'd lost ten pounds.

"Can you get me a coat hanger?" he asked when I walked in.

I grabbed one from the closet and tried to hand it to him.

"Not that kind," he said. "A wire one."

I found a hanger more to his liking and he took it.

"Thanks, cuz," he said as he unbent the hanger and slipped it under one of his plastic casts. "These things itch like a bitch and a half."

"How much longer do you need to wear them?" I asked.

"Five more weeks."

"That sucks."

"Tell me about it. It's only been eight days and I'm already going out of my mind. Between the itching, my mother, and all the legal mumbo jumbo I'm ready to join your mom in Shady Oaks."

"What kind of mumbo jumbo?" I asked.

"Papers, court filings, stuff like that. My lawyer's taking care of most of it."

"What does he think is going to happen?"

Roy set down the hanger and said, "A lot depends on Jackie's mom. She's some kind of born-again Christian and wrote off Jackie years ago. If she doesn't make a big deal about it, I might get away with a suspended sentence, or sixty days in County, tops."

"And if she does?"

"I'm hosed."

"Have you spoken to her?"

"My lawyer has. She says she'll pray for me."

"At least that's something," I said, and sat down beneath a poster of the New York Rangers from the year they beat the Canucks for the Stanley Cup. It was a little before my time, but Roy had a VHS of the series and used to watch it all the time. I've never understood the point of re-watching a game I've already seen, but Roy swore by it, and for years it was the only way he could fall asleep at night.

"How's the job with Mr. DeNunsio going?" he asked. "Dad said you were pissed off about having to step up."

"Just a little."

"Sorry. It's not like I planned any of this."

"What's done is done."

"Is it going okay?"

"So far so good," I replied. "I was hoping to have Vinny come along, but decided against it."

Roy leaned forward. "You didn't ask him, did you?"

"I was going to. Then we went out the other night, and he almost killed a guy at the mini golf in Deer Park."

"What happened?"

"I'm not sure. One second we were talking about you, and the next thing I knew he was strangling some guy with a golf club."

"That sounds like Vinny," Roy said with a laugh. "He's been wound a little tight the last couple of months."

"How come?"

"Too much meth. I don't think he's slept more than an hour since Labor Day."

A player scored a goal on TV, and we stopped to watch the referee disqualify the point.

"Give me a break!" Roy shouted. "There's no way that guy was offside."

"I didn't know you were a soccer fan."

"I'm not, but I watched the highlights from last night's Knicks game at least a dozen times, and those idiots on Sports Center were driving me crazy."

We stared at the TV in silence until out of nowhere Roy asked, "Do you think I'm going to Hell, Skip?"

"Why?" I asked.

"Why do you think? For killing Jackie."

"It's not like you meant to do it."

"Does that even matter? I was high, Jackie's dead, and now I'm charged with manslaughter." Roy lit another cigarette. "God, I hate that word—man*slaughter*. But that's what I did, Skip. I *slaughtered* her. She was so bloody and banged up it was like somebody had dropped her out of an airplane. I mean, look at my hands. Look at my face. They seem real, right? That's how Jackie looked until I hit that patch of ice, and then . . . slaughtered."

A commercial came on for a Spanish talk show, and we watched as a man in a tuxedo interviewed a grown woman in a cat costume. It made no sense and fit right in with the insanity of everything else in my life.

"Remember when Grandpa Patsy got sick?" Roy asked.

"Of course I do."

"Remember how he looked okay at first? I kept telling myself that if we just went about our lives and pretended like nothing was wrong the cancer would go away. Then he just got sicker and sicker."

"I remember."

"That's when I stopped going to see him. It was just too hard. But you never stopped, Skip. You kept going all the way to the end. More than Dad, more than your mom, more than all of us put together. Why did you do that, Skip? Why did you keep visiting him?"

"I don't know. I guess I didn't have anything better to do."

"That's bullshit and you know it. There had to be something else. I mean what did you guys talk about?"

"Nothing. Everything." I shrugged and said, "Mostly we just watched TV. Kind of like this, actually."

"Did he tell you anything special at the end? Anything memorable?"

"Not that I recall. He was pretty messed up on medication." I stood up and said, "I gotta go use the can."

I walked into the bathroom and tried to separate the real from the con. Roy was obviously torn up about Jackie, but the stuff about Grandpa Patsy? That was just a lame attempt to learn the whereabouts of Grandpa Patsy's money. I had to hand it to my cousin; even in his darkest hour he never stopped trying to scam people. That was forgivable, but bringing up Grandpa Patsy's death? That was off-limits, and I couldn't let it slide. I flushed the toilet and walked back into the bedroom.

"Speaking of Grandpa Patsy," I said. "Remember that time he dragged us to Our Lady of the Assumption during Easter week and made us confess everything to Father Burke?"

"Like it was yesterday, bro."

"You didn't do it."

"Sure I did."

I shook my head. "I was in the other confessional. All you said was that you disobeyed your parents and cursed. That was it. Nothing about stealing, nothing about lying, nothing about smoking weed."

"Who cares? Everybody smokes weed."

"I don't," I replied. "But all I'm saying is you didn't tell Father Burke your real sins."

"So?"

"You told Grandpa Patsy that you did."

"No, I didn't."

"I was *there*, Roy."

"Okay, so maybe I didn't tell the priest everything, but what's the big deal?"

"It's not a big deal," I replied. "I was just wondering if you ever thought about Grandpa Patsy looking down from heaven and knowing you lied to him."

"No, and why are you so sure Grandpa Patsy's in heaven?"

"Because he made a full confession. That's probably the

best thing about knowing you're going to die. You can get it all off your chest." Then I looked him in the eye and said, "Too bad Jackie didn't get the same opportunity."

Roy bit his lip, and I immediately regretted my words. Yes, it was uncool of him to bring up Grandpa Patsy, but bringing up Jackie was a total dick move. I thought about making it up to him by offering him something from my mother's medicine cabinet, but decided against it. The guy had enough problems without getting hooked on painkillers.

Besides, he probably sold them to her in the first place.

24

"WHERE'D YOU FIND THIS BOAT?" I ASKED THE NEXT afternoon when Mr. DeNunsio picked me up in an ancient Cadillac.

"I usually keep it in storage for the winter, but I had my guy drop it off at Shady Oaks in case I need to make a quick getaway. But it turns out it was a total waste of time because the deal's off."

"What? Why?"

"Because of this."

Mr. DeNunsio put the car in park and handed me a sheet of paper covered in numbers and percentages.

"What's this?" I asked.

"The results of a paternity test."

"Who's the lucky father?" I asked.

"Me."

I looked down at the sheet and said, "Aren't you a little old for this kind of thing?"

"I am now, but I wasn't seventeen years ago."

"Seventeen years ago? At that rate you could be my father."

"Not could be, Skip. Am."

I looked up, and there were tears in Mr. DeNunsio's eyes. My mind flashed to my mother, and the stories she told her therapy group, and I knew it was a scam.

"You sure about this?" I asked. "I mean, don't you have to take a blood test or something?"

"Not anymore. All you need is some DNA."

When I heard the letters DNA I had to bite my lip to keep from laughing. That was why Uncle Wonderful jammed that swab down my throat in the O'Neil Pavilion parking lot. It was all part of the con. A paternity test would tie me to Mr. DeNunsio by blood, which might make him trust me more. *Might* being the key word. Now it was my job to crank it up a notch.

"All it says is alleged father and child," I said, looking up from the paper. "This could be anybody."

"Did you give your uncle a DNA sample?" he asked.

"Not voluntarily, but yeah. How about you?"

He nodded. "I figured, why not?"

"You actually believe this?" I asked. "You know my family. They'd just as soon rip you off as tell you your shoe is untied."

"And when was the last time you met an honest criminal?" Mr. DeNunsio said with a laugh. "Anyway, I talked to the people at the lab. They assured me it was a hundred percent legitimate."

I shook my head. "I'm not believing any of this until we take another test without my family being involved."

"That makes sense."

I took out my iPhone and did a quick search on paternity tests. "Damn, it says here that the average turnaround time for a paternity test is five to seven business days. Even if we submitted the DNA tomorrow, we won't know the results until after I'm back at school." I handed the paper back to Mr. DeNunsio. As much as I wanted to quit this job, I knew my family would only come up with another one in its place. The best thing to do was just get it over with.

"Paternity test or not, I say we proceed."

"No," Mr. DeNunsio said. "I already lost two kids. I'm not losing a third."

"Do the numbers. Knowing my family, the odds that you're my father are like twenty percent. But the odds that Fat Nicky killed your family are a hundred. Where would you put your money?"

He sighed and said, "I don't know."

Then I delivered the clincher: "Besides, if it turns out that I am your son, I sure as hell want to kill the guy who killed my sisters."

He thought about it for a moment and said, "Okay, but

if things get hinky I reserve the right to pull the plug on the job until the last second."

"Deal."

Mr. DeNunsio put the car in gear, and we drove a circular route through Amityville and Copiague. When he was satisfied no one was following us he made a sharp turn in front of the Cheshire Arms Apartments. It had been years since I'd been in this neighborhood, and my mind flashed to riding my bike down Pine Wood Drive, and how I must have passed Fat Nicky's house a thousand times. I tried to picture myself back then, and what I would have said if someone told me that one day I'd be hired to kill the guy who lived there. I would have said they were crazy.

Mr. DeNunsio slowed down and said, "It's coming up on the left."

"The one with the humongous hedges?"

"That's it."

The house looked fairly nondescript considering the man who lived there was once one of America's top criminals. I don't know what I was expecting to see as we drove past. A moat? Gun turrets? For the most part, Fat Nicky's house looked downright cozy. I couldn't see much beyond the hedges, but the only things that looked out of the ordinary were a pair of floodlights mounted on high poles on either side of the yard.

Mr. DeNunsio said, "I can't tell you how many times I've driven past this house. It's like a magnet for me. I'd tell myself I was just going out for cigarettes, or to gas up the car, and then I'd always end up here. I knew it was stupid, but I couldn't help myself. I guess deep down I always knew I'd try and kill the bastard."

We drove to the end of the block, made a couple of turns, and parked in a marina facing the Great South Bay. Mr. DeNunsio turned off the engine, and we stared out at the water as he gave me my final orders.

"Do it while you're on the clock at the Pavilion so you'll have an alibi. The whole thing shouldn't take more than an hour. Wear latex gloves and something dark. Slip out, do the hit, and come back. Remember, you gotta shoot him twice in the head. He got lucky last time, but if his brains look like a pile of scungilli, you know he's history."

"How many men have you killed?" I asked.

"Four."

"Does it ever bug you?"

It took him a long time to answer, and I watched through the windshield as a seagull dove into the water and came up with a fish in its mouth. *See that*, I told myself. In the animal kingdom everyone's a murderer.

"One guy still bothers me," Mr. DeNunsio finally said. "The other three? It was their own fault. They knew the rules and they screwed up. But the other guy . . . that one still gets to me." He pulled out his inhaler and lit a cigarette. "It was right after my first hit, and I felt like God Almighty. I was leaving a bar, and this kid snuck up behind me and stuck a gun in my back. I should have just let him take my wallet, but I was a cocky punk back then. After he took off, I went back to my car, grabbed a tire iron, and a-hunting I did go. I found him a few blocks away counting my money. He never saw me coming. I smashed his arms. I smashed his legs. I can't remember half of what I did. But I'll never forget the expression on his face right before I brought the tire iron down for the last time. He had this look of wet fear in his eyes that I still see in my dreams. Or should I say nightmares?" He sighed and flicked his cigarette out the window. "Ain't that a kick in the head? He's the only one who did something to me personally and he's the one I still feel guilty about."

We drove away in silence, and I tried not to dwell on Mr. DeNunsio's story. After all, if he beat a guy to death for taking his wallet, what would he do to me for stealing his life savings? Maybe that's why my family had stuck with petty crime for all those years. Maybe deep down we were all just a bunch of lightweights who couldn't take the pressure.

It didn't seem like a smart idea to take a bus to a murder, so I had Mr. DeNunsio drop me off near Roy's apartment. I had been lusting after a bike like Roy's for days, but had remained honest and not stolen one for myself. Stealing Roy's bike, on the other hand, barely qualified as theft. Besides, with both his legs broken, it wasn't like he would need it any time soon.

I climbed the stairs to Roy's apartment, and as I reached the second floor I heard the thump, thump of a stereo cranked up super loud. Talk about a lucky break. It was just what I needed to drown out the sound of me breaking into Roy's apartment. Then, as I got closer, I realized the music was coming from *inside* Roy's apartment. This made no sense because Roy was back at Uncle Wonderful's house, so I peeked in the window and saw Roy and Vinny sitting on the couch. They had big grins on their faces, and a woman in cowboy boots was dancing in front of them. I couldn't see her face, but she was wearing a short skirt and a Shooters' belt, and I turned away out of embarrassment. There was something about a woman performing exclusively for Roy and Vinny that struck me as ten times creepier than Jackie dancing for a room of drooling idiots at Shooters. Then I realized Roy didn't have any casts on his legs and when I turned back to double-check I saw that the woman dancing for Roy and Vinny *was* Jackie.

Ice water shot up my spine, and it took all my self-control to keep from screaming.

This can't be possible, I told myself. *If Jackie is alive that means there was no car accident—*

And if there was no car accident that means Roy isn't really hurt—

And if Roy isn't really hurt, then there's no reason for me to be doing this job—

Unless, I was supposed to be doing this job all along, which meant—

I was being set up.

My brain shifted into high gear, and I tried to figure out who else was involved in the con: Roy, Vinny, and Jackie, obviously. And Uncle Wonderful, too. But who else? My mother? Aunt Marie?

And what about Mr. DeNunsio? He was supposed to be the mark, but if there was one thing I'd learned growing up in a family of con artists, it's that if you're not 100 percent sure who the mark is, then the mark is probably you.

Someone changed the song on the stereo, and I realized it was time to get out of there. I ran down the stairs and slipped around back to the parking lot. I spotted Vinny's Hummer in a handicapped spot and was tempted to smash his windows with a brick. But that would have been stupid, and the last thing I needed in my life was more stupidity. I'd been wallowing in it for days, and it was time to wise up.

It was either that or get conned, killed, or both.

25

THE FIRST TIME ROY AND I PLAYED CRASH IT WAS A GOOF—just a couple of juvenile delinquents messing around on bikes—but the more we played, the more competitive we became. Which is a nice way of saying crazier and way more dangerous. The time Roy broke his wrist is the perfect example. One of us got the bright idea to ride our bikes on train tracks, and the other agreed. For those of you who have never tried it, riding a bicycle on train tracks is right up there with sticking pebbles in your ears or playing with matches as A Really Dumb Thing to Do. First off, you have to ride your bike over railroad ties, which is like totally impossible. Second, you have to stand up the entire time, or it's like getting punched in the nuts every two seconds. And third, you can get hit by a train.

The way we got around the railroad tie and nut-busting part was to cut the tires off our bikes and ride directly on the train rails. This is infinitely more difficult than it sounds, and the hardest thing about it was getting started without falling over. That's how Roy broke his wrist. But here's the amazing part: After Roy broke his wrist he didn't say a word. He just got right back on his bike and fell over three more times before he finally got going. Can you imagine landing on a broken wrist not once, but *three* times? It must have been excruciating, but Roy didn't even grunt. Which was why I should have known something was wrong when I visited him after the accident and he complained about his leg itching. Complaining just wasn't Roy's style.

Crash was definitely on my mind that night when I took a bus to the Sunrise Mall and stole a bike from the rack behind H&M. Yes, I know I said I wasn't going to do it, but with Roy's bike being guarded by a couple of drooling potheads and a formerly dead Shooters' girl, I had no choice. Locks had grown more sophisticated since the last time I had stolen a bike, but auto parts stores still sold air-conditioning coolant, and in less than two minutes I was pedaling away on this totally sweet Trek DS. Just for old time's sake, I rode past the Macy's where my mother and I were arrested and stopped by the Burger King for a soda. It had been over a decade since I'd been there, and as I waited at the drive-through I wondered—for perhaps the millionth time—what it would take to get away from my family forever.

The easiest thing to do, I realized, would be to kill them. I had a gun, and more than enough ammo, so what was stopping me? Only everything. Still, the more I thought about it, the more appealing it became. Shooting Uncle Wonderful was a no-brainer. I already despised him, so it was simply a matter of following my bliss. Shooting Roy and my mother, on the other hand, would be hard. Then it hit me. Maybe I only needed to shoot Uncle Wonderful for my mother and Roy to understand how serious I was. And if push came to shove, I could always pump a couple of bullets into Roy's knees to prove I wasn't fooling around. Sure, then afterward I could rob a bank, hijack a yacht, and become a pirate.

Okay, so there was no way I was shooting anyone, but somewhere between ordering my Dr Pepper and picking it up at the drive-through window, an even better idea came to me. I had asked Mr. DeNunsio to get me a Walther PPK because it was the only gun I knew. But what if, instead of taking Mr. DeNunsio's gun to Fat Nicky's, I took Uncle Wonderful's gun instead? That way, if something went wrong, I could leave Uncle Wonderful's gun for the police. I could even plant a few strands of his hair around the crime scene for extra bonus points. Now here was a plan I could get behind, and as much as I would have enjoyed dressing up like a pirate and sailing the seven seas, this seemed a lot more doable.

With Uncle Wonderful out of the picture, it was time to focus on the other two members of my family. I dialed my uncle's house, and when Aunt Marie answered I said, "This is Skip. I need to talk to Roy right away."

"He's not here right now," she said before her brain kicked in. "Wait, I mean he's asleep. That's right, he's asleep."

"Okay," I said, trying not to laugh. "Do me a favor, and tell him I'll be over tomorrow afternoon around one."

"Sure, Skip. I'd be happy to."

My next stop was Shady Oaks, and as I pedaled across town a wave of sadness washed over me. I didn't care that Uncle Wonderful had set me up, but it really hurt that Roy was part of the deal. I know it sounds corny, but I would have given anything to play Crash with him one last time. Unfortunately, that was never going to happen. During the time when I had grown a conscience, Roy had just grown hard. And cousin or not, I was the guy who had stolen the imaginary millions he thought were his.

I took a detour through Massapequa Park and rode under the elevated train tracks as the train to New York City pulled into the station. I looked up at the concrete stanchions and every intelligent cell in my body told me to forget about Claire and Princeton and get on that train and never look back.

The only problem was I couldn't. I'd chosen my path, and the best I could do was race the train to the next station. I started out in the lead, but the train caught up fast and beat me by a mile.

It took a long time for me to catch my breath after I had stopped pedaling, although this was probably because I was crying so hard. Roy, Aunt Marie, Uncle Wonderful.

They were all against me now. And the more I thought about it, the more I knew my mother was, too. Talk about being careful what you wish for. I'd been trying to get away from my family since I was thirteen years old, and now that I was almost there, I felt scared and alone. And young. Really young. It's embarrassing to admit, but even after I took Grandpa Patsy's money, I still told myself I could return home if things got bad. But now things were bad, and it was my family who was making them that way.

Then I thought of something else and stopped crying. Yes, my family was against me, and yes there was a strong chance that if I went through with the job they still wouldn't leave me alone. Except I was smarter than they were, and the only reason I had fallen for their little scam was that I was out of practice. I'd been thinking like Cam Smith when I should have been thinking like Skip O'Rourke. That ended now. As much as I hated to admit it, Jackie was right. I *was* like them.

But here's the thing: I was also enjoying myself. I had stepped up to the challenge of out-weaseling my family, and not only was I good at it, it was some of the most fun I'd had in a long time. And since I had zero choice in the matter, I figured it was time to enjoy myself a bit more.

No more Campfire Girl stuff for me.

26

THE ANGRIEST I EVER SAW MY MOTHER WAS THE TIME SHE got ripped off by her card club. We were living in Elizabeth, New Jersey, in this dinky apartment complex filled with a bunch of old retired ladies who had all worked at the same oil refinery in Linden. They were a tight-knit and cliquish group, and we had an impossible time making friends with them. This was a problem for a couple of reasons. First off, my mother prided herself on being able to talk to anyone, and when she couldn't strike up a conversation with the Ladies from Linden—as we began calling them—it was a major blow to her ego. Second, and far more important from a business perspective, was that if we couldn't talk to them, we couldn't rob them.

Mom and I tried every trick we knew to ingratiate ourselves with the Ladies from Linden, but after three weeks with zero success we were about to give up. Then, out of nowhere, Mrs. McGreevy from the fourth floor asked my mother if she wanted to play cards that night with "a few of the girls."

"It's just a penny-ante thing," she assured us. "More BS-ing than cards."

My mother agreed immediately, which surprised me. After watching Grandpa Patsy throw away every nickel he stole betting on football and basketball games, my mother despised gambling. I was even more surprised, however, when we went back to our apartment, and she broke out the playing cards.

"Sit down," she said, cutting the seal on the deck with her thumbnail. "I need to practice."

Over the next few hours, my mother taught me everything she knew about poker. She started off easy, but by the time we were finished with Five-card stud, Texas hold'em, and Follow the Queen my head was ready to explode.

"Where did you learn this stuff?" I asked in exasperation.

"Uncle Wonderful and I used to play all the time when we were kids. Watch this." She fanned the deck with one hand and pulled out the five of clubs with the other. Next, she placed the five on the top of the deck, shuffled the cards, and put the deck in front of me.

"Take the card off the top."

It was the five of clubs.

"Good. Now put it back." She shuffled the cards again and said, "Now take the card off the bottom."

It was the five of clubs again.

"How did you do that?" I asked.

"A good magician never reveals her secrets," she said with a grin. She showed me two or three other tricks, and by the time she was through, I was convinced my mother was the greatest card player in the world.

Which was why I was so surprised when she came home from her card party looking like she wanted to cry.

"What's happened?" I asked.

"I lost sixty-two bucks."

"I thought it was penny ante. That's like six thousand, two hundred pennies."

"I know how many pennies it is, Socrates," she growled. "I don't know what happened. It wasn't like any of them were particularly good card players, but they just kept winning. I don't get it."

The same thing happened the next week, except this time she lost eighty-one dollars. Her luck improved the week after that when she won twelve dollars, but then she lost fifty-three and seventy-one dollars in the following two weeks.

"You're being taken," Uncle Wonderful said when he heard her story.

"That's impossible," my mother replied. "I've been watching those biddies like a hawk, and nobody's doing better than anybody else."

"That's because you're looking at it the wrong way. It's not you against four individual biddies. It's four biddies teamed up against *you*."

My mother's eyes grew wide and she slammed the table with her fist. "Son of a bitch! That's how they did it. How could I have been so stupid?"

"Face it, Sheila. You always were lousy at cards."

"Shut up, Wonderful."

I don't know what made my mother angrier, the fact that she lost a few hundred dollars or that Uncle Wonderful had figured out the scam first. Either way, by the following week, we had it all worked out. While my mother went to Mrs. McGreevy's apartment and lost another fifty-four dollars, I went to the other ladies' apartments and stole everything they treasured. But that was far from the end of it. Even though she never set foot in New Jersey again, my mother spent the next two years doing everything imaginable to make the lives of the Ladies from Linden a living hell. She scrawled their phone numbers in truck stop bathrooms, ordered dirty magazines in their names, and had their phone and cable service downgraded, upgraded, or cut off entirely. It was ridiculous.

"Why are you still doing this?" I asked after the joke had been ground into dust a dozen times over. "It's not like you haven't been ripped off before."

"Yeah, but those old bags did it for fun."

"What difference does that make?" I asked.

"A lot," she replied. "Think about it, Sonny. Every one of those women is collecting a pension, Social Security, and God knows what else. They don't *need* the money. Ripping me off was a game to them. A lark. They saw this dumpy woman with stretch pants and a bad perm and thought they could take me for a ride. They thought I was a sucker and that they were better than me. Well, guess what? They might have won the first round, but they won't win another."

This was how I knew my mother was part of Roy's scam. She may have missed me when I ran away, she may have even loved me, but she could never forgive me for stealing Grandpa Patsy's money. So, like the cable service and multiple subscriptions to *Playboy* that she showered upon the Ladies from Linden, the car, the house, and the suicide attempt were all part of an elaborate con to get back at me. I knew this instinctively. The only problem was, I still loved my mother, and all those years of the two of us crammed into crummy apartments, living on frozen pizzas, and watching *Judge Judy* on our stolen Trinitron forged a bond between us that even revenge couldn't completely erase.

But knowing's not enough, and like Grandpa Patsy used to say, there's nothing more useless than an understanding criminal. Which was why I got out the box containing my mother's good name, made copies of everything inside, and shipped the originals to Wheaton. It wasn't the greatest insurance policy in the world, but it was better than nothing. I just hoped it was enough to save my life when my family made their move against me.

27

STEALING UNCLE WONDERFUL'S GUN WAS EASY PEASY. WITH Roy strapped in his fake casts, and Aunt Marie and Uncle Wonderful at Lowe's fighting over discount lighting fixtures, their bedroom was wide open. It took less than a minute to pull on a pair of latex gloves, hop on a stepladder, and steal the gun from the closet.

I slipped the Walther into a Ziploc bag and was about to take a few strands of hair from the brush on Uncle Wonderful's nightstand when I spotted his backup false teeth. They were sitting on his dresser like a couple of dusty clam shells and upon closer inspection I saw that each pair had a unique serial number etched on top. They were perfect. Not only were the teeth covered in Uncle Wonderful's DNA, but fake name or not, the serial numbers would lead the police straight to him. I stashed a pair of teeth in the Ziloc along with some hair and a can of maximum strength jock itch spray I found in the bathroom.

When I got back home, I ran some water through the coffeemaker and squeezed a couple of drops of Crazy Glue into the carafe. I held the jock itch can over the steam, and a dozen fingerprints appeared like magic. Most were smeared, but two were perfect, and unless Aunt Marie had a sex change operation while I was off at Wheaton, the fingerprints were definitely Uncle Wonderful's.

I waited for the glue to dry and carried the can, gun, and battery-powered UV light I'd bought at the local spy store into a closet. I turned on the light and compared the fingerprints on the gun to those on the jock itch can. There were three good prints above the grip and two more on the barrel. I concentrated on the barrel because it would be impossible not to smear the prints above the grip if I was forced to pull the gun on Fat Nicky. I glanced back and forth between the gun and the jock itch can until I was certain the prints belonged to Uncle Wonderful and not Roy or Aunt Marie.

My next task was to try on my wet suit. I had never worn one before and I'd learned from the salesman at the dive shop that the best model for late December water was something called a 5/3. These numbers stood for the thickness of the layers of neoprene used in the suit's construction, and meant it could be worn in water as cold as 45 degrees. Considering that the average late December water temperature was in the low 40s, this was the suit for me.

Unfortunately, they didn't have a 5/3 in my size. I could have bought a larger one, but the salesman warned me that a badly fitting wet suit is almost as bad as no wet suit at all. I wound up settling for a 4/3, which was rated for water temperatures down to 50 degrees. This was a little worrisome, but I figured I'd only be in the canal for ten or fifteen minutes and I'd just have to suck it up and deal.

I packed the suit, false teeth, and gun in my backpack, and when it got dark outside I went out to steal a Honda Accord. Long Island is Accord Heaven and nobody pays the slightest bit of attention to them. It took less than twenty minutes to find one without a kid's car seat in the back and another two minutes to pop the door and crack the ignition. After that, it was simply a matter of changing the radio station and topping off the gas tank.

I parked the Accord in the garage and went to take a nap. I was too cranked up to sleep and spent the next two hours going over the job in my head. In the past, I'd always been the thief-in-training, but this time the entire job rested on my shoulders, and I was overwhelmed. I once asked Grandpa Patsy what it felt like being an adult, and he just laughed and said, "Two words, Skip: more responsibility." I now understood what he meant, but I still didn't feel like an adult. I felt like a kid about to steal his first bag of M&M's.

The doorbell rang, and I sat up in bed. No one beside my family knew where I was, and there was no reason for them to be paying me a visit. That left a neighbor, a kid selling cookies, or the police. I could have ignored the first two, but the last thing I needed was a cop parked in the driveway when I pulled out of the garage in a stolen Accord.

I hid the Walther behind a throw pillow in the living room, took a deep breath, and opened the door.

"Cam?" Claire said, her face pinched with confusion. "What's going on?"

I was too shocked to reply and just stood there with my mouth hanging open.

"Aren't you going to answer me?"

"What was the question again?"

"What the hell are you doing here? You said you were at school."

"Funny you should mention that . . ." I began, but the rest of the words died in my mouth. Yes, I could have concocted some outrageous story, and yes Claire might have believed it. But then what? More stories? More lies? No, I was through telling lies. It was one thing to deceive my family, who wouldn't have recognized the truth if it whacked them over the head, but I couldn't lie to the one person I truly loved. It was time to come clean, and if Claire didn't accept me for who I was . . . Well, at least I tried.

"Come on in," I said, taking her hand. "I want to show you something." I led her to my bedroom and showed her my wall of awards.

"Who are all these people?" she asked. "I don't recognize any of the names."

"They're me," I replied. "They're all me."

"I don't understand."

So, I told her. I told her everything. All the way from my very first break-in straight to the hot-wired Accord in the garage. I held back nothing and spared no one, especially myself. I thought it would be painful, but it turned out to be the opposite. To finally get all those lies and stories off my chest was the most liberating thing I had ever done. Claire stayed silent through my entire saga and never once interrupted. I had no idea what she was thinking, and I eventually stopped caring because it felt so good to make a full and complete confession.

When I was finished, I looked Claire in the eyes and asked, "Any questions?"

"Only a million," she said, and her gaze came to rest on my wall of awards. She stood up to examine them more closely and without looking back at me asked, "Cam, if you're so good at lying, how can I ever trust you? I mean, how do I know I'm not just another security guard you're fast talking?"

"Because this is different. Think about it. You're the first person who knows who I really am who hasn't tried to steal my Social Security number." Claire didn't respond and I said, "What I mean is, I love you. And I think—*I hope*—you love me."

"That's the problem," she replied. "I fell for someone named Cam Smith and now I find out he's really named Skip O'Rourke. Or," she pointed to one of my awards. "Is it Stephen James? Or Matthew Trezza? Or Martin Grant?"

"I'm me," I said, placing a hand on my chest. "I'm the same person I've always been. It's just that . . . It's just that—"

"What?"

I got up and stood next to her. "Do you remember what it was like to be thirteen years old?"

"Yes."

"Do you think you could have done what I did and leave everything you knew behind?"

"Of course not. I was just a kid."

"And I wasn't?"

"You were," she said, turning away. "But you were also a thief and a liar."

Claire's words were the equivalent of a guilty verdict. I sat down on my bed and tried to think of the right thing to say, but it was useless. I could talk for a million years, and it would never erase where I came from. I was a liar and a thief, and that's who I would always be. And now that Claire knew my story it was ridiculous to think she would see me as anything else. My family had won without even trying. But I couldn't let them claim victory without a fight and said, "Look, Claire, I know I've messed up big time, but is there any way we can fix this?"

"We can start by never lying again."

"It's too late. As far as Wheaton and Princeton are concerned I'm Cam Smith. It's a done deal."

"I understand that, but you have to promise never to lie *to me* again."

"Of course I'll never lie to you again. I never wanted to lie to you in the first place."

Claire turned to me with an expression I couldn't quite read. "And I promise I'll never lie to you again."

"What are you talking about?"

She looked down at the ground. "I never finished my Princeton essay."

"That's okay," I said, not understanding why she was so upset. "There are still a couple of days left before it's due. We can work on it together if you want."

"Cam, I didn't finish my essay because I never started it. I don't want to go to Princeton. I never even applied."

"Never even applied? That doesn't make sense."

But of course it made sense, I thought as anger tore through my veins. It made *perfect* sense. I fell in love with a girl, and she lied to me. It was the story of my life.

Claire said something, but I didn't hear her as I sprung up and began pulling the awards off the wall. What was the point of yellow ribbons and calligraphy-covered certificates? What was the point of *anything* if I couldn't trust anyone? If every word was a lie, and every emotion a weakness to be exploited?

"Stop it!" Claire yelled. "You're not the only one trying to start over."

"What the hell is that supposed to mean?"

"Exactly how it sounds. You look at my life and see this wonderful thing to aspire to, but all I see is this endless future of drunken affairs and Junior League rummage sales. I want to get away from my family just as much as you want to get away from yours."

"Your family is nothing like mine," I said. "And besides, not everyone who goes to Princeton turns out like your parents. F. Scott Fitzgerald went to Princeton."

"And he drank himself to death."

"Okay, so maybe he isn't the best example—"

"Listen to me, Cam," Claire said, and took my hand. "Princeton was your dream, not mine. It always has been."

"It's not a dream without you," I said.

"That's bullshit! And if I thought for one second you really believed that I'd walk out on you right now."

"Isn't that what you're doing? Walking out on me?"

"No. I'm just not going to Princeton. My parents are going to be furious about this. Please don't be pissed off at me, too. I'm sorry to be dropping this bomb on you now, but I didn't make up my mind until I went home."

"But you had to be thinking it."

"Yes, and I felt like I was being unfair to you the entire time. And you know what the worst part was? The more excited you got about Princeton the more horrible I felt."

"Why didn't you just say something to me?"

"I didn't know how until you told me about your family, and then I realized we're kind of going through the same thing."

I tried to picture Princeton without Claire, and everything went from color to black and white. "What are you going to do if you don't go to school?" I asked.

"I'm not sure yet." Then a smile crossed her lips and she said, "Maybe I can work at Home Depot."

"That's *so* not funny," I replied.

"Aw c'mon," she said, poking me in the ribs. "You have to admit it was a little funny."

"No, it wasn't."

"I thought you said you'd never lie to me again?"

"Okay, fine. It was a little funny. Are you happy?"

"Delirious."

And that's when we kissed.

Later, as we were lying under my *Star Wars* sheets and basking in the post Possibility of Expulsion glow, I asked Claire how she had found me.

"Remember that picture you sent me a few days ago? I was looking at it this afternoon and noticed Han Solo and Chewbacca in the background. I'd never seen these sheets on your bed at school so I looked up the metadata on the photo, and it said you were here. It seemed like a mistake, so I turned on the Find My iPhone app, and that said the same thing. It made no sense why you would lie to me about where you were, and I didn't know if you were dealing drugs, or if there was another woman, or what."

"You're right," I said. "There is another woman in my life. It's just that she's my mother."

"Even after everything you've told me about her, I almost wish I could meet her."

"Why would you want to do that?"

"Because she's your mother, and you're my boyfriend, and it's kind of the normal thing to do."

"But my family isn't normal. They're a pack of weasels."

Claire laughed. "You say it like you don't love them."

"Of course I love them. They're just better loved from a distance of a few hundred miles."

"Do you really think they'll leave you alone after tonight?"

"Probably not, but I think they'll let me finish Wheaton if I go through with the job. Right now that's the best I can hope for."

The alarm on my iPhone chimed telling me it was time to go. I got up to look out the window and saw that it was snowing.

"Damn it," I said.

"What's the matter?"

"The storm got here earlier than it was supposed to. Riding my bike in this weather is going to suck."

"I can drive you."

"I appreciate the sentiment, but the last thing you need is to get involved in my family's nonsense or get arrested. Stuff like that follows you around the rest of your life."

"My father was arrested, and it turned out okay for him."

My mind flashed to the life-sized Ken doll I'd seen in the Wheaton parking lot and shook my head. "That's impossible."

"Okay, so technically he was only indicted, but it's practically the same thing."

"Why was your father indicted?" I asked.

"He develops real estate for a living. Sometimes projects require money, kickbacks, or other . . . things."

"What kind of other things?"

"Bribes, jobs for idiot nephews, you name it. One time he even hired a hooker for a city councilman. When my mother found out about it she didn't talk to him for a month. So you see, Skip, your family isn't all that different from mine."

"I wouldn't go that far."

"You can go as far as you want, but you need help, and I'm going to help you."

I closed my eyes and tried to clear my head. The only intelligent change to make to a plan at the last minute was to abandon it entirely, but that wasn't going to happen. I had to go through with the job, and as much as I hated involving Claire I needed her help.

"Okay," I said, opening my eyes. "Let's do this."

"All right."

"But first," I said, reaching for my iPhone, "could you turn off that Find My iPhone app? The last thing we need is anyone knowing where we are tonight."

28

NOW THAT CLAIRE WAS PART OF THE JOB, MY CHALLENGE was to keep her exposure to a minimum. The original plan had been to park the Accord near The Cheshire Arms and ride my bike back and forth to Shady Oaks. Claire drove instead, and by the time we got to Shady Oaks there was an inch of snow on the ground. If that wasn't bad enough, according to the weather app on my iPhone the storm was sending ice-cold water into the canals. It was going to be a frosty night.

I clocked in for my shift and after I checked to make sure no patients were wandering the halls, I pulled out a ladder and set all the clocks ahead two hours. This wasn't the most sophisticated trick in the book, but if a patient happened to see me and was later called to testify, they might—I repeat, might—say I was at Shady Oaks at 2:00

a.m. instead of at Fat Nicky's. Sometimes it's the little things that wind up saving you.

Claire's revelation about not going to Princeton totally destroyed my ability to focus, and I couldn't shake the feeling that I had forgotten something. I stopped by Mr. DeNunsio's room for a glass of anisette I didn't drink, but it was something to kill the time because I was nervous, nervous, nervous. My mind kept bouncing between Claire and the job and the job and Claire, and at some point I realized Mr. DeNunsio was whistling the same three notes over and over.

"Will you cut that out!" I barked.

"Why?" he asked. "What's the matter?"

"What do you think is the matter? I'm scared."

"You should be. Killing a man is scary business."

I swished the anisette around in the glass and said, "I've been thinking. Maybe I'm the wrong guy for this job."

"No, you're the right guy."

"How do you know?"

"Because, son or no son, you had the stones to say yes."

I sat on the edge of Mr. DeNunsio's bed. "And another thing. Fat Nicky's an old man. Realistically, how much time does he have left? Two years? Three? Maybe we should let him slide."

"Not in a million years," Mr. DeNunsio replied with dead certainty. "If he had only one minute left to live. I'd take it away from him in a heartbeat."

"Why?"

"You want to know why? I'll tell you why." He sucked on his inhaler and lit a cigarette. "The night before I put my family in the ground, I got drunk and broke into the funeral home. And there they were. Three coffins. Two big and one small. Ever see a kid's coffin?"

"No," I whispered.

"Well, let me tell you, it's the saddest thing in the world. And drunken fool that I was, I opened it. God help me for doing so, but I had to see what was inside. You know what was in there?"

I shook my head.

"A shriveled up foot in a black patent leather shoe. That's it. One foot. That was all that was left of my baby." He blew some smoke out of his nose and said, "Any more questions?"

"No."

"Good."

There was nothing left to say, and we stared at our glasses in silence. Then, in the distance, I heard the sound of metal tapping on glass.

"What's that?" Mr. DeNunsio asked, looking up.

"I don't know. But I better go find out."

But I knew exactly who it was. It was Claire dropping by to say she had changed her mind! She had decided to apply to Princeton after all, and all her talk about affairs and rummage sales was a mistake. Her timing couldn't have been worse, but I didn't care and raced down the hallway to meet her. I skidded into the lobby, but instead of finding Claire I found Frank. He was leaning against the door and banging his keys against the glass. He looked drunk, stoned, or some combination of the two.

"The Pavilion's closed," I said. "Come back in the morning."

"I know the Pavilion's closed. Let me in."

"Sorry. It's against the rules."

"Screw the rules," he slurred. "And when did they change the locks?"

"Right after they fired you. Now get out of here before I call the cops."

The C-word made him take a step back and he said, "Okay, but do me a favor, will you?"

"What?"

"You know Sal DeNunsio in room 128?"

"Yeah?" I croaked.

"Next time you cross paths tell him I said hello. Okay?"

"Tell him you said hello?" I repeated in a lifeless voice. "Anything else?"

"No. That's it."

Frank walked away, and I raced back to Mr. DeNunsio's room. There had to be a reason for Frank to appear out of nowhere, and my anxiety-riddled brain latched onto the most obvious reason I could find.

"You had a visitor," I said, throwing open the door.

"Who?"

"Frank."

Mr. DeNunsio looked confused. "Frank? Who used to work here? What did he want?"

"He said to tell you hello. Now what do you suppose that means?"

"I don't know. What do you think?"

I knew just what it meant and grabbed a fork off the nightstand. I jammed it against his throat and said, "You asked him to kill Fat Nicky first? Didn't you? Didn't you?"

Mr. DeNunsio barely blinked. "I said think, not go crazy. Now be a good boy, and try to use your brain for a second. Why do you think Frank got fired?"

"For stealing drugs."

"And why did that happen?"

"He said somebody didn't know how to keep their mouth shut."

"Right. And who do you think that somebody was?"

I thought about it a moment and said, "You?"

Mr. DeNunsio smiled. "Bingo."

"Why did you do that?"

"So I could spend some quality time with members of the O'Rourke family."

I exhaled loudly. "Ohhh . . ."

"Now, will you do me a favor and take that fork away from my throat before I soil my dignity pad?"

I set the fork on the nightstand and said, "I'm sorry, Mr. DeNunsio. I totally freaked out."

"Don't worry. It happens to everyone. Now hold out your hands and let me see how steady they are."

I held out my hands, and Mr. DeNunsio slapped me across the face.

"You little punk," he growled. "I don't care if you are my kid. You threaten me again, and I'll tear your fucking lungs out."

I put a hand to my cheek and it felt hot.

"Did that hurt?" Mr. DeNunsio asked.

"Of course it hurt."

"Good. A little pain keeps you on your toes. Now get the hell out of here and go kill that bastard."

Seeing no alternative, I picked up the empty glass of anisette and headed for the door.

"Oh, and Skip?"

I turned around, and Mr. DeNunsio was holding up his hand like a gun.

"Remember. Two in the head."

29

THIRTY MINUTES LATER I WAS COVERED IN DARK BLUE neoprene and diving into the icy waters behind the Cheshire Arms Apartments. The Accord was parked two blocks away, and Uncle Wonderful's gun and false teeth were in a Ziploc in my backpack. Claire, meanwhile, was sitting in her BMW at a Taco Bell in Amityville. The plan was for me to steal the picture, swim back to the Accord, and meet up with Claire who would drive me back to Shady Oaks. A fast food restaurant wasn't the best place in the world to ditch a getaway car, but it was a safe place for Claire to wait, and therefore a good compromise.

I had never jumped into freezing water before, and even with a neoprene hood covering two-thirds of my head, it was like getting smashed in the face with a block of ice. My lungs contracted and my testicles shot so far up my gut I thought they would shoot out of the top of my head. Ice-cold water slipped into the nooks and crannies of my wet suit, and I began to shiver. I tried to warm myself by swimming as fast as I could, but between my tensed up muscles and contracted lungs it was slow going.

"Why didn't they have a thicker suit?" I asked the darkness, but the darkness didn't answer, and I kept swimming until I reached Fat Nicky's dock.

I grabbed onto an aluminum ladder and as I pulled myself up I half-expected a dog to bark, or a security light to pop on. Nothing happened. This should have been my first clue that something was wrong, but I was too cold and scared to give it much thought. There was a large glass window at the back of the house, and as I moved toward it I was struck by how normal it looked inside. It could have been my house or Uncle Wonderful's or anyone's. A TV was on, and the light from the screen danced over the furniture and walls.

I followed the light across the room, and that's when I spotted the man I'd been hired to kill. He was asleep in a recliner with a newspaper in his lap and his mouth hanging open. I stared at him for what felt like an eternity, but no matter how long I stood there he just didn't seem capable of the crimes Mr. DeNunsio had described. Then again, I didn't look like a professional killer, so I guess that made us even.

I slunk to the back of the house, and my heart thumped harder with every step. I pulled a penknife out of my backpack and with surprisingly little effort popped the lock on a side window. It had been years since I'd broken into a house and I felt out of practice, but once inside, it was just like old times. My eyes adjusted to the light, and as I swapped my neoprene gloves for a latex pair I saw that I was in a bedroom. Like the rest of the house it looked as normal as normal could be. I got the gun out of my backpack and clicked off the safety. Even through my gloves the gun felt colder than death, and as I made my way into the living room I had to breathe through my nose to keep from hyperventilating.

Easy does it, I told myself. *And no matter what happens, don't do anything stupid.*

A bald head poked over the back of the recliner, and a plastic tube ran from the chair to the oxygen tank beside it. I spied the picture of Frank Sinatra hanging over the TV, and as far as prized possessions went, it was pretty underwhelming. I took a deep breath and made a wide arc around the recliner, keeping my eyes on Fat Nicky the entire time. He didn't grunt, snore, or fart, and I reached out for the picture. It came off the wall with ease, and I was about to slip it in my backpack when the telephone rang.

"What the hell—" Fat Nicky said.

I spun around, and as I aimed my gun at Fat Nicky things began to make sense. The house. The car. My messed-up financial aid. They were all distractions to keep me from figuring out the real plan, which was for me to kill the man sitting less than five feet in front of me. The key to the entire charade was the part about faking Fat Nicky's death. It was so stupid in an O'Rourke-kind-of-way that my family knew I would fall for it.

Fat Nicky rose from his recliner, and I pointed the gun at his forehead.

"Sit down, old man," I said in the toughest voice I could muster.

He settled back in his chair and looked me up and down. "Okay," he said in a weary voice. "Who sent you?"

I was too busy figuring out my next move to answer his question. The person who had made that phone call knew exactly when to do it, which meant that either Roy or Uncle Wonderful was outside watching my every move. They must have thought I'd freak out and shoot Fat Nicky the moment the phone rang. Or that he'd shoot me. Either way, they'd get what they wanted, which was money or revenge.

"C'mon, kid," Fat Nicky said. "The least you can do is tell me who's putting up the capital to have me killed."

Funny you should mention that, I wanted to reply. *Because I was thinking the same thing.*

"You want to know something?" he said. "I've been sitting in this chair for over a decade waiting for you to come. When you didn't show after the first couple of years I started to think you weren't coming, and that maybe they forgot about me." He started to laugh.

"What's so funny?" I asked.

"I never thought you'd be so young and innocent looking. Are you toilet trained yet, baby?"

"Keep your hands where I can see them, and you can call me whatever you want. Just remember, I'm the person who's going to hear your last words, so if you have something memorable to say, you should be nice to me."

"You're smart with your mouth, but you're not too smart doing a job. If you were, I'd be dead already."

"And miss all this great conversation?"

Fat Nicky smirked and said, "It was Martinelli who hired you, wasn't it?"

"No."

"Pozzaglia?"

"Sorry."

"Juliano?"

"Not even close."

"Who was it then? I give up."

"Mr. DeNunsio."

Fat Nicky blinked. "Who the hell is that? I don't know any DeNunsio."

"His nickname was Sally Broccoli."

"I don't know any Sally Broccoli, either."

"You killed his family in the eighties."

"What are you talking about? I never killed anybody."

"What about those guys in that restaurant in Bay Ridge? The newspapers said you killed two of them."

"I haven't been to Bay Ridge in, like, twenty years. I think you broke into the wrong house, kid."

I held up the picture and said, "Then why does the person standing next to Sinatra look so much like you?"

“Because it is me. So what? Last time I checked that wasn’t a reason to shoot a guy.”

“No, but blowing up a man’s family is.”

“Blowing up a—Hold on a second. Who do you think I am?”

“Fat Nicky Gangliosi.”

“The mobster? I thought he was dead.” The oxygen tube fell from his nose, and he reached up to adjust it.

“Put your hand down, or I’ll shoot you in the stomach.”

“Fine. Go ahead and shoot me. But I’m still not Fat Nicky Gangliosi.”

“Then who are you?”

“Louie Jingo.”

“That name means nothing to me.”

“Big deal. I’ve never heard of you either.”

But what he said made sense. The wide open backyard, the big picture window, the absence of bodyguards. Retired or not, no former mob boss would ever leave himself so vulnerable.

“Open your shirt,” I said.

“Excuse me?”

“Open your shirt. Fat Nicky was shot in the chest. If I don’t see any scars, then I know you’re not him.”

He did as I asked and his chest was clean.

“Happy?” he asked.

“Overjoyed.”

“Just out of curiosity,” he said, buttoning his shirt, “how much are you getting to take me out?”

"Four hundred bucks."

Louie Jingo's jaw almost fell in his lap. "Are you kidding me?"

"Why?" I asked. "Is that too little?"

"Abso-freaking-lutely. I should be worth at least twenty times that. Tell you what. Let me pay you ten grand, and we can forget all about this."

"It's not about the money," I replied. "It's about my freedom."

"Bullshit. If there's one thing I've learned in this world, it's whenever somebody tells you it's not about the money, it's *all* about the money."

"Not for me."

Fat Nicky snapped his fingers. "Now I know why I never heard of this Sally Broccoli character. He's subbing you out."

"What's that?"

"A subcontractor. Somebody hired him to do the hit, and he hired you to do it for him. How'd you meet this guy, anyway?"

"In a nursing home."

"Retirement money!" he said with a laugh. "This guy's a beaut. Somebody pays him twenty Gs to whack me, and he slips you four hundred and hightails it to Miami Beach."

"No way."

"Believe what you want, kiddo. You're being had. Sally Broccoli? Gimme a break." Then his eyes grew wide and he shouted, "Now, Vito!"

I turned to see if someone was behind me as Louie Jingo

jumped up and grabbed the end of my gun. It was a good move and might have worked if his fingers didn't get caught up in the hose for his oxygen tank. I pulled the trigger, and he flew backward, hitting his head on a table.

"Jesus Christ," he screamed. "You shot me."

"No, I didn't. That was just muzzle flash."

Louie Jingo pulled his hand away from his chest and saw it was clean. "You're right," he said.

"Unfortunately, your head is another story."

He ran his hand through his hair and his fingers were red with blood. "Damn, that really hurt."

"You'll live," I replied as I picked up a pillow and wrapped it around the barrel of the Walther.

"What are you doing?" he cried.

"Saving both our lives."

"Wait a minute, I—"

I aimed the pillow above his head and pulled the trigger three times fast. The pillow made an excellent silencer, but I forgot about the feathers, and they filled the room like the snowstorm outside.

"That was stupid," I said, wiping a feather from my face.

"Are you out of your mind?" Louie Jingo hissed.

"Stop moving," I said. "You're supposed to be dead."

I lowered the gun and looked around. "You have a first aid kit someplace? I need to patch up your head."

"What do I look like? A park ranger?"

"I guess we'll have to improvise. But first I need to get you away from that window so whoever's out there thinks

I really killed you." I grabbed his ankles and said, "You know what I still don't understand? If you're a nobody, why would somebody pay twenty thousand dollars to have you killed?"

"Because a long time ago I stole something."

"What?"

"Two million bucks."

I let out a low whistle. "Two million. That's pretty sweet."

"Biggest mistake of my life."

"Why?"

"I didn't know it at the time, but the money was meant for a government sting operation. The job went bad, and by the time the dust settled, I had the Feds after me, the guys I robbed after me, and my ex-partners after me, too. So, as far as people wanting me dead, the list is as long as your arm. Just out of curiosity, what does this Broccoli guy look like?"

"Old, kind of tall, walks with a couple of canes."

"And let me guess. His knuckles are covered with scars."

"How'd you know?"

"Because his real name is Chaz Martinelli and he was one of my partners on the heist. I had really hoped the son of a bitch had died."

"How come he changed his name?"

"Because he shot a treasury agent in the leg, and cops tend to have long memories about stuff like that."

Now the con—with all its twists and turns—was coming into focus: Louie was lying low with the stolen money, and Chaz was hiding out from the Feds. He'd changed his name to Sal DeNunsio and at some point had a fling with my mother. Years later, my mother found out her old boyfriend was living at Shady Oaks and figured she'd con him out of his life savings. She lost some weight, got herself committed, and tried to convince Chaz I was his son. The only question remaining was whether my family was conning Chaz, or if Chaz was conning my family.

I dragged Louie Jingo into the kitchen with his oxygen tank still hooked to his nose and pulled a dish towel from a drawer. As I bandaged his head, I realized that he and I had something in common. We both had people who wanted to kill us for money we stole.

"And you know what the saddest part of my story is?" he asked.

"What?"

"The money was worthless. It was less than worthless."

"Why?"

"The bills were marked. I tried to pass a couple and I nearly got pinched by a dozen treasury agents."

"Do you still have it?" I asked.

"What? The money? Only an idiot would hold on to something like that."

"You didn't answer my question."

Louie Jingo smiled. "Of course I still have it. I went through hell getting that money and I'll be damned if I was just gonna throw it away."

"Good," I said, seeing a chance to get away from my family once and for all. "Because I want half of it."

30

ONCE LOUIE JINGO'S HEAD WAS BANDAGED, I HAD TO MOVE fast. I didn't know if Roy or Uncle Wonderful were still outside, and as much as I would have enjoyed flipping them off, I had more important things to do. Like getting out of there alive, for example. I drew the curtains over the big glass windows, and while Louie Jingo dug out his good name and made plans to leave Long Island permanently, I grabbed a couple of big plastic garbage bags and filled them with towels, frozen hamburger, and everything else I could find that looked like a dead body. After that, I smeared Uncle Wonderful's gun and false teeth with Louie Jingo's blood and stuffed them in a Ziploc bag. Then, for my last and most important trick, I dragged the bags across the backyard and dove into the canal with them clutched in my arms.

The key to everything was for my family to believe I

had actually killed Louie Jingo. Lucky for me, the tide was going out, and the waves took the "body" with them. Unlucky for me, I had left my neoprene gloves at Louie Jingo's house. I thought I could tough it out instead of going back for them, but by the time I got back to the Cheshire Arms my hands were swollen and burning with frostbite. I managed to drive the Accord to the Taco Bell, but if Claire hadn't picked me up I never would have made it back to Shady Oaks.

"Oh my God," she shrieked when I emptied out my backpack and she saw the Ziploc bag with the gun and teeth. "You didn't—"

"Kill him? No."

"But that blood. It has to belong to someone."

"Oh, it certainly does."

As we left Taco Bell, I told Claire about Louie Jingo, and how my family planned for me to kill him. From the expression on her face I could see that the gravity of my situation had finally become real to her. This wasn't just a bunch of rich developers indicting one another for fun and profit. It was life and death.

"What are you going to do?" she asked. "Those people—your family—they're still out there."

"I know, and that's why I need you to do something for me. It's a little dangerous, and if you don't want to do it I totally understand."

"What is it?"

"I need you to go to Louie Jingo's house, pick up a million bucks, then go back to school and wait for me."

It was hell changing out of my wet suit in the front seat of the BMW, but fifteen minutes later I slipped into the Williams Pavilion and raced to the employees' restroom. My hands were still swollen and throbbing, and I held my fingers under warm water to take the edge off the pain. It was just starting to fade when someone knocked on the bathroom door.

"Skip?" came a voice from the hallway. "Are you in there?"

"Yes?"

"It's Valerie from the O'Neil Pavilion. You better come quick."

"What is it?"

"A nurse found your mother on the floor of her room. They think she had a stroke."

I followed Valerie to the O'Neil Pavilion, and when we got to my mother's room it was like stumbling upon the scene of a car accident. A doctor, three nurses, and a pair of technicians were circling her bed and shouting at one another in rapid-fire medicalese. My mother looked completely out of it, but when I grabbed her hand her eyes lit up, and she made a croaking noise.

"What did she say?" I asked the doctor.

"I'm not sure, but it's probably not what she intended. Garbled speech is a common symptom in these situations."

"Is it permanent?"

"Too early to tell. We're just lucky the nurse found her

when she did. If it is a stroke, the sooner she's treated the better."

"When did it happen?"

"We can't say exactly, but judging from her condition no more than an hour."

An hour. Right about the time I was supposed to kill Louie Jingo. There was a clattering behind me and two paramedics rushed in with a gurney.

"What's going on?" I asked.

The doctor flashed a light in my mother's right eye and said, "We're taking her to the hospital for a CT scan. Once we assess the extent of the bleed—if it is a bleed—we'll know if we have to operate or not."

"And if you do?"

"It's going to be a very long night." He flashed a light in her left eye. "You need to wait outside for the next few minutes. After that, you can ride with her in the ambulance."

"Okay," I said, and headed toward the door. Then something occurred to me, and I turned back to the doctor.

"Is it possible to fake a stroke?" I asked.

The doctor stopped what he was doing and looked at me like I was the one who belonged in a mental institution. "Maybe," he said. "Why?"

"Just curious." I glanced at my mother, and she quickly looked away. Bingo.

I stepped outside, and Valerie was waiting for me.

"How's she doing?" she asked.

"The doctor's not sure yet."

"It's a good thing they found her when they did. With stroke victims the sooner they're treated the better."

"That's what he said."

Valerie scanned the hallway. "I'm surprised your Uncle Wonderful isn't here." She grabbed the chart hanging next to the door and flipped it open. "He's listed as her next of kin. They should have called him the minute they found her. It's the law."

That's because he was too busy trying to get me killed, I wanted to reply. Instead I asked, "Who should have called him?"

"The nurse on duty."

I was 90 percent sure Uncle Wonderful was the person who had been hiding in Louie Jingo's backyard, but I needed proof and dialed Uncle Wonderful's house on my iPhone.

"Hello?" answered the scratchy voice of my aunt Marie.

"This is Skip. I'm sorry for calling so late, but is Uncle Wonderful there?"

"No, the bastards took him away."

"What bastards?" I asked. "Who took him away?"

"The Federal Bureau of Idiots, that's who."

"The FBI? What did they want?"

"How am I supposed to know? You think Wonderful tells me anything? He could be the president of the United States, and I wouldn't know about it until two weeks after the inauguration."

"When did they take him?"

"This morning while I was out shopping. They waited for me to leave so there wouldn't be any witnesses if he fell on his way out the door."

"Have you spoken to him?"

"No, he called his lawyer, and his lawyer called me."

"I'm really sorry, Aunt Marie."

"What do you expect? You play with fire long enough and sooner or later you get burned."

"Did the people from Shady Oaks call?"

"Yes, that's terrible news about your mother. I have a doctor's appointment tomorrow at nine fifteen, but I'll try to drop by and see her after that."

I pushed End and stared up at the ceiling. Damn. Bloody gun or not, with Uncle Wonderful in federal custody there was no way I could frame him for killing Louie Jingo. Talk about the perfect alibi. There were probably a dozen people who could have vouched for his whereabouts every second of the last fifteen hours. Add to that video surveillance, police logs, and other irrefutable evidence, and my plan was totally shot. Who would have thought that getting arrested by the Feds could turn out to be a good thing?

"Hello, son."

I turned, and Mr. DeNunsio was standing beside me. My first impulse was to kick his canes out from under him, but there were too many witnesses around. Instead I bit my lip and kept my feet planted firmly on the ground.

"I'm sorry to hear about your mother," he said. "I came as soon as I heard. How's she doing?"

"The doctors say it's still too early to tell."

"Thank God they found her. The thing about strokes is the faster they treat you the better."

"So I've heard."

He took a step closer. "What about that other thing? Everything work out okay?"

"Check your garbage can," I said.

"What?"

"The garbage can in your room. Go look inside it."

His eyes grew wide. "Why?"

"Because there's only one glass there. Remember when you slapped me across the face? You were so full of yourself you didn't notice I took your glass with me. A friend of mine has it now, and it's got your fingerprints all over it. So listen up. If anything funny happens to me—and I mean anything—that glass and the gun that did the job go straight to the cops. *Capisce?*"

Mr. DeNunsio glared at me.

"So where's the picture?" he asked after a moment.

"I didn't see the point in taking it."

"Why?"

"Because my cousin Roy saw everything. You want proof? Go ask him."

The paramedics wheeled my mother out of the room, and I slapped Mr. DeNunsio on the back. "Thanks for the anisette, Chaz."

I followed the paramedics down the hallway and straight out the front door. There was an ambulance waiting, and I watched as they rolled my mother inside. I climbed in beside her, and the paramedics closed the door and pulled out. There was an IV bag hanging from a pole on the gurney, and I followed the tube down to my mother. She was staring at me with large, questioning eyes, and I smiled.

"Hello, Dolores," I said.

She blinked.

"That's your name, isn't it? Dolores Spencer? Or should I say your *good name*?"

She said nothing, but I could tell she wanted to.

"Just so you know, I have it all. The license, the passport, the Social Security card. Don't worry; it's all in a safe place. In fact, it's in the same place as a pair of Uncle Wonderful's false teeth, a glass with DeNunsio's fingerprints, and the gun that killed Fat Nicky. That's right. If one of us goes down, we all do. Any questions?"

She didn't answer, and I leaned in closer.

"And just so we're clear, after we get to the hospital, you and I are finished. If you try to contact me in any way—and I mean so much as a birthday card—I'm giving that package to the police. Got it?"

She still didn't answer, and I was beginning to think that she really did have a stroke. Just to make sure I said, "And in case you're wondering, I'm the one who stole Grandpa Patsy's money. I've had it in a storage locker upstate the entire time."

"You son of a bitch."

"What's that?" I asked, putting a hand to my ear.

"You heard me," she growled as she grabbed my throat. It happened so quickly I had no time to defend myself, and the paramedics in the front of the ambulance didn't hear a thing. Her thumbs dug deep into my Adam's apple, and I tried to pry her fingers away, but my hands were still useless from the cold. She was killing me. I couldn't believe it. My own mother was killing me.

Things were getting fuzzy fast. I thought about praying, but decided against it. I had chosen my path, and it was time to pay for my choices. I kept my mind focused on Claire and tried to picture what it would have been like growing old together. I saw beaches and sunsets, horses and rainbows. Yes, I know it sounds corny, but I was too busy dying to paint a *Mona Lisa*. Everything went black, and just when I thought my life was over, someone grabbed my ankles and pulled me out of the ambulance.

"Are you okay?" a paramedic asked, snapping an ammonia capsule under my nose.

"What?" I replied, still not fully conscious.

"I said, are you okay?"

I heard my mother scream, and everything came rushing back. I scrambled to my feet and peered inside the ambulance. A second paramedic was strapping my mother to the gurney, and she was kicking and screaming like an insane woman.

"Will you look at that," I said with a cough. "Is that the world's fastest stroke recovery, or what?"

31

I JAMMED THE GUN I GOT AT RED LOBSTER INTO THE BACK of my pants and climbed the stairs to Roy's apartment. My hands were throbbing and my throat felt like I'd gargled with drain cleaner, but I was alive. Or at least I was for a few more minutes. I still wasn't sure what to do about my cousin. Half of me wanted to shoot him, and half of me wanted to give him a high five for pulling off such an outrageous scam. But what I really wanted was to get as far away from Long Island as possible, which was exactly what I planned on doing once I was finished with Royston Patrick O'Rourke.

Music was blasting from his apartment, and I peered through the curtains to see if Jackie was in the middle of another performance. Not even close. Roy was asleep on the couch with a beer in one hand and a bong in the other. I thought about kicking my way inside but decided against it. If Roy did have a gun, the last thing I needed was to spook him. I gave the door a friendly knock, and when he didn't answer, I gave it a not-so-friendly punch.

"Who is it?" he yelled.

"Your favorite cousin."

The door opened, and Roy appeared holding a baseball bat.

"Hello, Killer," he said.

"Getting ready for spring training?" I asked.

"This is for protection."

"From who? Me?"

"Maybe."

"I have a gun, Roy. If I wanted to kill you, you'd already be dead."

Roy tossed the bat on the couch and said, "Then I guess you might as well come in."

I followed him inside, and the first things I noticed were two plastic casts on the floor.

"How are the legs doing?" I asked.

"Good as new."

"And Jackie?" I asked, collapsing on a chair.

"What about her?"

"Are you two, like, dating?"

"I don't know. I mean, she's hot and everything, but the girl has serious anger issues." He sat on the couch and fired up a bong.

"So, now what?" I asked.

"What do you mean?" he asked, releasing the smoke into the room.

"Is this thing over, or not?"

"Of course it is. Fat Nicky's dead."

"No, he's not."

"Bullshit. I saw you cap the guy."

"That wasn't Fat Nicky."

"Then who was it?"

"Some nobody named Louie Jingo."

Roy leaned forward. "You mean DeNunsio double-crossed us?"

"Don't look so surprised," I said. "It's not like he was the only one getting double-crossed last night."

"Sorry about that. If it was up to me, I would have gotten somebody else to do the job, but Dad and your mom had their hearts set on you."

"Just out of curiosity, when did you guys figure out I was at Wheaton?"

"About thirty seconds after you left. We knew your good name, so it wasn't that hard."

"Then why did you wait so long to come and get me?"

"Dad was waiting for the right job. But honestly, I think your mom wanted to make you think you got away with it. Life sucks, huh?"

"What's done is done," I said. "What I really want to know is whether you guys are going to leave me alone now."

"You're family, Skip," Roy said with a smile. "You know that's impossible."

I reached into my pants and pulled out the gun.

"Is that supposed to be some kind of a threat?" he asked.

"No, it was poking me in the kidney. But if you'd like, it could be a threat."

Roy shook his head. "I'll pass."

"Suit yourself, but we still have to figure out some amicable way for you to leave me alone for the rest of my life."

"It's not just me. It's the entire family."

"Let's not worry about them right now."

Roy thought about it for a moment. "If it's just the two of us, then maybe there is a way to work things out."

My face erupted into a grin. "Are you thinking what I'm thinking?"

"Bikes or cars?" Roy asked, grinning back.

"If this is a fight to the death, then we better make it cars."

It took less than an hour to find what we needed. I stole a Camaro 2LS, and Roy opted for a Challenger SXT. We switched license plates, pulled the air bags, and loaded up on gas and munchies at a Citgo station. My hands were still a burning mess, but I figured the adrenalin and insanity would pull me through.

"What's the plan?" Roy asked, biting into a microwave burrito. "Where do you want to do this thing?"

I checked the time on my phone. "It's almost nine a.m. Unless you want to get civilians involved, we'll have to find a place where there's no traffic."

"This is Long Island. All we got is traffic."

I thought about it and said, "What about Ocean Parkway? Nobody's going to the beach this time of year."

"Good idea. We can race from Jones Beach to Captree State Park. The first person to die loses."

Roy climbed into the Challenger, and I followed him down Sunrise Highway and onto Wantagh Parkway. Traffic was nonexistent, and we blew past the Jones Beach tollbooths, skidded around the water tower, and hit Ocean Parkway doing eighty.

I had been dreaming of this moment for years and couldn't wait to make the first move. I cut my wheel hard to the right and plowed straight into Roy's fender. He gave me the finger, and I was about to nail him again when he hit the brakes. I had zero time to react and smashed into the Challenger with my gas pedal pressed to the floor. Pain shot up my neck as my head snapped forward, and I almost bit off the end of my tongue. Roy blasted his horn and was gone before I could even look up.

"You son of a bitch," I screamed.

My mouth filled with blood, and I guzzled some soda and spat it out the window. As bad as my tongue hurt, my pride hurt more. I couldn't believe I had fallen for such a sucker move. We may have been equal on bicycles, but Roy had way more experience behind the wheel of a car.

I hit the gas and aimed the Camaro straight for him. The car inhaled the distance between us, and I was just inches from his bumper when he slammed on the brakes again. This time I was ready for him and cut my wheel hard to the left. I shot past Roy doing eighty, and in less than a minute I was a quarter mile in the lead. The Camaro shook like an unbalanced washing machine, and I prayed it would hold together long enough for me to get out of there. I'd been planning to send Roy to a ficry grave, but my new strategy was to stay as far ahead of him as possible and either outrun him or bore him to death. I was hoping for the latter when a voice came over the Camaro's sound system.

"This is OnStar operator Kevin. This vehicle has been reported stolen, and the police have been notified. We are currently in the process of disabling it."

"Wait a minute!" I shouted. But it's impossible to size up a mark you can't see, and I tore open the glove compartment in search of the car's registration.

"Are you still there?" I asked.

"Yes, I'm here."

"That's great. Uh, Kevin was it?"

"Yes."

"That's a great name, Kevin. In fact, you're not going believe this, but my father's name is Kevin."

"You're right," he replied. "I don't believe you."

The words ENGINE POWER REDUCING flashed on the dashboard, and the Camaro began to slow down. I checked the rearview mirror, and Roy was racing up behind me.

"Listen," I said. "How do you know the person who reported this car stolen was the actual owner and not some knucklehead pulling a prank?"

I dumped the contents of the glove compartment onto the seat beside me. The registration had to be there somewhere.

"Because he gave us his account number."

I slapped the dashboard and said, "Now I know what happened. I lost my wallet at a Rangers game last month, and my account number was in there. My wife must have forgotten to call you. Can we update my information now, or is that something I have to do at the dealership?" I found the registration and almost died when I saw the name on it. "I mean, what do I have to do to convince you I'm . . . Magnus Kjartansson."

"It's pronounced K-JARtansson," Kevin said with a snort.

"That's what I said."

"No, it wasn't."

So much for fast-talking my way out of the situation.

I checked the rearview mirror, and Roy was practically on top of me. Worse, a cop was practically on top of him. The Camaro was losing power by the second, and my only hope of escape was abandoning the car at Cedar Beach, which was coming up fast. The turn into the parking lot was crazy sharp, and I had serious doubts that my frostbitten fingers could handle it. I hit the brakes and slapped the steering wheel with the palms of my hands. Time stood still, and I hit a divider and crashed into a boarded up parking booth. The booth exploded, and wood and wire flew everywhere as I bounced into a parking lot and slammed into a sand dune. I held my breath and waited for Roy or the cop to race in behind me.

But nothing happened. Nothing at all.

I got out of the Camaro and climbed onto the sand dune to see where everyone was. I shielded my eyes from the sun and saw Roy racing down the parkway with the cop on his tail. This meant either Roy couldn't make the turn or had decided to try and outrun the cop. Either way, I wasn't waiting around to see if they were coming back. I buried my gun in the sand, wiped down the Camaro for prints, and dashed across Ocean Parkway to the westbound lanes.

There was very little traffic, and I slogged through marshes and sea grass until I came to the town of West Gilgo Beach. Most of the houses were closed for the winter, but a few looked occupied, and one of them even had a Honda Accord parked in the driveway.

"Wow," I said, not believing my eyes. "Today must be my lucky day."

32

I SPENT THE NEXT TWO WEEKS LOOKING OVER MY SHOULDER and poring over the Long Island papers for news about my family. I didn't expect to find anything about my mother, but I figured there might be a piece about Uncle Wonderful and the FBI, or Roy getting nabbed in a high speed chase. There was nothing, and unlike the rest of the world where no news is good news, in the land of thieving weasels, no news means it's time to start checking for the knife in your back.

My fears were finally realized on the third Monday of January. Maybe it's just me, but if there's anything more nerve-racking than seeing the woman who'd tried to strangle you appear at your school's Martin Luther King Day Celebration I have yet to find it. But there she was, third row center, wearing a big smile and an even bigger hat, which—even I had to admit—looked terrific on her. In fact,

I couldn't remember another time when my mother looked so good, and if it was any other day, I would have been happy to see her. Sadly, this was also the day I was supposed to meet Claire's parents, and I didn't want my mother to do anything embarrassing, like stealing their wallets.

Once I was able to pry my eyes off my mother's hat I spotted two familiar faces sitting next to her: Roy and Uncle Wonderful. As flattered as I was that my entire family had come to watch our Senior Class Reading of Martin Luther King's letter from a Birmingham jail, something told me they weren't just there for the civil rights. I debated ducking out the back door or faking an epileptic seizure, but neither of these struck me as the kind of first impression I wanted to make on Claire's parents, who were sitting just three rows behind my family.

Any way you looked at it, I was trapped.

Claire was seated at the opposite side of the stage, and there was no way for me to signal her. I didn't think my family would do anything stupid as we stood and marched down the center aisle at the end of the reading, but I was forced to reevaluate this opinion when Roy sleazed up behind me and stuck either a gun or a roll of Mentos in my back. I was hoping it was the latter because my mouth had suddenly gone dry and I could have used something to freshen my breath.

"Meet us at that statue of the guy and the dwarf," he whispered.

"It's not a dwarf," I said. "It's a child."

"Whatever. Just meet us there, or I'll shoot you in the ass."

"With all these people around? You wouldn't dare."

"Do you really want to risk it?"

"My entire life has been one endless risk. Why should today be any different?"

"Just meet us there."

The statue in question was of Archibald Wheaton, our school's founder and first president. Old Archie, as everyone called the statue, was a popular spot for late night hookups and family introductions. To the best of my knowledge it had never been the site of a murder or shooting, and my goal was to keep it that way. And just my luck, it was also where I was supposed to meet Mr. and Mrs. Benson.

We filed out of the building, and as we gathered on the Great Lawn to light candles and sing "Amazing Grace" I rushed up to Claire.

"My family's here," I whispered.

"You mean *here* here?" She turned to face the crowd coming out of the auditorium. "Where?"

"Stop looking around so much. I don't want them to see me talking to you. Can you pick me up behind the storage facility in fifteen minutes?"

"Of course."

"What about your parents?"

"I'll tell them to meet us at the restaurant. Are you going to be okay?"

"I'm not sure, but I don't have much of a choice."

I squeezed Claire's hand and raced toward the dorms. It took Roy less than a minute to catch up and guide me to the visitor's parking lot where we were joined by the rest of my family.

"I'm so proud of you," my mother said, giving me the world's biggest hug. "That presentation was incredibly moving."

"Thanks, Ma. Coming from you that really means a lot."

I glanced past her and smiled at Uncle Wonderful.

"Hello, Skipper," he said.

"Hi, Uncle Wonderful. Did the Feds give you the day off, or did you sneak out of jail in a laundry hamper?"

"The Feds never had me, you rube. I can't believe you actually fell for that."

"Me neither," I said with a sigh.

My mother let go of me, and I turned to face my cousin.

"So, Roy, was that cop who chased you down Ocean Parkway bogus, too?"

"No, the cop was real. Lucky for me, I lost him in the boat basin. Vinny had to come and rescue me."

"How is the Vinster?" I asked.

"In rehab."

"Glad to hear he's finally getting his act together."

"Not even close. It was either that, or ninety days in County. Now he's dealing meth to the other patients and making more money than ever."

"Enough catching up," Uncle Wonderful shouted. "Tell us where your storage space is."

I took a deep breath and said, "Storage space? What storage space?"

"The one you told me about in the ambulance," my mother replied. "You remember, dear."

"You mean right before you tried to strangle me?"

"That's right."

I pretended to debate the pros and cons of telling them the location when Roy pulled out his gun and said, "C'mon, Skip. I have tickets to a Rangers game tonight."

"Fine," I said. "But I get to keep a quarter of the money."

"You get nothing," Uncle Wonderful hissed. "Now tell us where it is, or I'll have Roy shoot you right here and now."

I made a move like I was going to knock the false teeth out of Uncle Wonderful's mouth, and Roy grabbed me from behind.

"Don't even think about it."

I pulled myself free and said, "Fine. It's ten miles south of here in Rensselaer. Get on the Northway, and I'll show you from there."

My mother and Uncle Wonderful climbed in the front of the car, and Roy and I got in the back. We pulled out of the parking lot, and I looked out the rear window to see my entire class singing "Amazing Grace." I should have been there with them, and that's when it struck me that my family's biggest crime wasn't scamming welfare checks or stealing DVD collections. It was robbing me of a childhood.

Wheaton disappeared in the distance, and I turned to

face my mother. “So, did you really date Mr. DeNunsio, or was that a lie, too?”

“Really, Sonny. What kind of question is that?”

“I think it’s pretty straightforward.”

“Maybe,” she said with a shrug. “But he wasn’t the only man I was seeing at the time.”

“Let me guess. The other two were a diesel mechanic and an Irish tenor.”

“Am I the one telling this story, or are you?”

“Sorry.”

She brushed my apology away and said, “It doesn’t matter anyway. The only thing that mattered was that Sal was living at Shady Oaks, and there was a possibility you could be his son.”

“Don’t you mean Chaz?”

“Who’s Chaz?” my mother asked.

“Nobody,” I replied. “Nobody at all.”

And that was the final piece of the puzzle. My mother had no idea who her old boyfriend really was which meant that Chaz had been running the show all along. He must have seen my mother’s con coming from a mile away and came up with the story about killing Fat Nicky so my family wouldn’t guess his true identity. My mother took the bait, Uncle Wonderful dragged me back to Long Island, and they set me up to kill a man.

Anger flared up inside me, and I debated jumping out of the car. We were going sixty miles an hour and I might have gotten killed, but it was better than spending another moment with my family. I checked the sideview mirror, grabbed the door handle, and—

Nothing happened.

"Kiddie locks," Uncle Wonderful announced. "They keep the little ones from falling onto the highway."

My family had thought of everything.

Five minutes later we pulled off the Northway and I said, "See that big blue sign coming up on the right?"

"Yeah."

"That's the place. Go around back. It's locker number seventeen."

It was total overkill to rent a ten-by-twenty-foot storage locker to hide a pair of bags that could have easily fit under my bed, but the storage facility was only an eighth of a mile from Interstate 90. If things went south, I could make a run for it and be on the highway in less than two minutes.

"How much you paying for this thing?" Roy asked as we pulled up to the locker.

"One hundred and forty-three a month plus tax."

"You're getting robbed. My friend Johnny Gillespie would have charged you less than a hundred."

"I'll have to remember that next time I need to hide something from you."

"Just open the damn thing already," Uncle Wonderful growled.

I climbed out of the car, and Roy followed me with his gun at my back.

"Do you really need that?" I asked.

"Yes."

"Don't do anything silly, Sonny," my mother called out. "I'd hate for something bad to happen to you."

I glanced back at my family and could almost see the saliva dribbling down their chins. They'd been waiting for this moment for years, and each of them thought they deserved what was inside that locker.

And you know what? They were right.

I pulled up the door and a shaft of sunlight revealed two duffel bags sitting in the middle of the room. "There they are," I said. "Knock yourselves out."

Uncle Wonderful stepped forward. "No, you open them."

"Suit yourself."

I unzipped the first bag to reveal the money, and a couple of feathers floated out.

"Holy macaroni," my mother said. "There must be a million bucks in there."

"One point two, to be precise."

My family stood there speechless, and for a moment I thought they were going to dive in the bag and start rubbing the money all over themselves. I took advantage of their distraction to take a step closer to the second bag. Two more steps, and I could grab it and be on Interstate 90 before they knew what hit them.

"Let's split it up now," Roy said.

"No," my mother and Uncle Wonderful said simultaneously. "Back at home."

"Then at least give me one stack," Roy said. "I'm going to the city tonight."

My mother shook her head. "Not until we count it and decide how to divvy it up."

"What's to decide?" Roy asked. "One point two divided three ways is four hundred grand each. Subtract ten Gs for the stack I'm taking to the city, and that's four hundred for you two, and three hundred and ninety for me."

"Who said we were splitting it evenly?" Uncle Wonderful said.

"Wait a minute!" Roy shouted. "I'm entitled to just as much as you are."

This was my opening, and I grabbed the second bag. I turned to run, and the next thing I knew I was lying on the ground with blood pouring from my nose. I looked up, and my mother was rubbing her fist.

"You shouldn't have done that, dear."

"Why not?" I asked. "It's what you would have done."

"Do as I say, and not as I do," she said, and took the bag from my hand. She opened it and pulled out two Ziploc bags. One contained Uncle Wonderful's gun and Mr. DeNunsio's glass, and the other contained her good name.

"You should really take better care of your things," she said, handing the Ziploc with the gun to her brother.

Uncle Wonderful stared at the bloody Walther with a combination of fear and awe. "Damn," he said. "You really killed that guy. I didn't think you had it in you."

"At least somebody in this family does."

"We'll see about that," he said, and pulled the gun from the Ziploc bag. He checked to make sure it was loaded and turned to my mother.

"Get in the car, Sheila. Put the money in the trunk and wait for me."

Roy and my mother did as they were told, and Uncle Wonderful aimed the Walther at my chipped tooth. I stared down the barrel and wondered if there was another way I could have played my hand, if there was something else I could have done to escape from my family without stealing Grandpa Patsy's money.

"Just out of curiosity," I asked. "Do you think we would have ended up like this if I had stayed on Long Island?"

"Woulda, shoulda, coulda," he replied. "Besides, you were never really one of us."

I didn't think Uncle Wonderful had the guts to shoot me, which was why I was almost as surprised as he was when he pulled the trigger. Lucky for me, the gun was still loaded with the blanks I'd put in it on the night I went to "kill" Fat Nicky. As Uncle Wonderful stood there dumbfounded, I reached into a darkened corner of the storage locker for my lacrosse stick. This time it was right where it was supposed to be, and I knocked him to the ground with one swing. I heard a car door open and spun around to see Roy racing toward me with his pistol. I took a step to the right, and as he raised his arm to fire, I swung my lacrosse stick and caught the gun in the net.

"Okay," I said, grabbing the gun and pointing it at him. "Get in the locker with your father."

"Look, Skip, I—"

"Save it, Roy. I shot Louie Jingo, and I'll shoot you, too." Then I turned to my mother and said, "Get out of the car and get inside the locker."

"Thank God you're all right, Sonny. I don't know what I would have done if something bad happened to you."

"Just get in the locker."

After they were all inside, I grabbed the door handle and said, "A guard comes by every ninety minutes. Bang loud and he'll find you."

"What about the money?" Roy asked.

"Keep it," I said. "It's a down payment for leaving me alone the rest of my life."

My mother started to say something, but I didn't want to hear it and pulled the locker door shut. I was tempted to break the key off in the lock, but thought better of it and ran behind the storage facility to where Claire was waiting for me in her car.

"Are you okay?" she asked.

"They tried to kill me," I said. "My own family tried to kill me."

"Jesus!" Claire said. "I had no idea they'd do something that crazy." Then she wrapped her arms around me and said, "If it's any consolation, I promise my parents won't try to kill you."

"That's reassuring," I said, and Claire put the car in gear.

From the *New York Post*:

FBI Nabs Three Crooks in Decades-Old Heist

This morning Federal agents announced the arrest of two suspects in a 1995 robbery and shooting of an undercover agent. Philip O'Rourke, 57, and Sheila O'Rourke, 53, were apprehended in predawn raids in Copiague and Amityville. Also arrested was Royston Patrick O'Rourke, 22. All three possessed bills from the robbery which they had only recently begun spending. Agents say the case was cracked when the younger O'Rourke dropped over ten thousand dollars in marked bills at a Manhattan strip club.

If convicted, Philip and Sheila O'Rourke face a maximum of twenty-five years to life in prison for the shooting of a federal agent, while Royston O'Rourke is looking at five years for possession of the stolen cash, not to mention being an idiot. When asked why the trio would wait over ten years to pass the money, Special Agent Richard McMahon replied, "They're a pack of weasels. Who knows why they do what they do?"

ACKNOWLEDGMENTS

Uwe Stender, my agent at TriadaUS, is the greatest guy in the world and the reason you are reading these words. Brent Taylor, also at TriadaUS, is the most enthusiastic reader imaginable and a fantastic agent in his own right. Namrata Tripathi, my editor at Dial Books for Young Readers, is a gift from the literary gods and made this book far better than I ever thought possible. Stacey Friedberg, also at Dial, is a backstage ninja with a black belt in awesomeness. David Liss is the best friend a writer could ever have. Period. My wife, Anne, deserves to bathe in a tub filled with diamonds every night for all the help she gave me with this project. My children, Liam and Kate, fill me with joy and giggles on an almost hourly basis. And Mom, I miss you terribly.

BILLY TAYLOR is the author of the adult novel *Based on the Movie*. He is a graduate of the Film Program at SUNY Purchase and the Interactive Telecommunications Program at New York University. Before turning his hand to writing, he worked as a dolly grip on dozens of movies and TV shows, including *Pee-Wee's Playhouse* and *My Cousin Vinny*. He lives in San Antonio, Texas, with his wife, Anne, and two amazing children, Liam and Kate. Visit him online at billytaylor.com.